The Third Book of THE MODERATOR

Grid Lock

DWIGHT KOPP

Grid Lock – Copyright ©2014 Dwight Kopp

ISBN 978-0-9895853-6-1

Cover Design by Dwight Kopp
Cover Image Power Button © MS Media

For Doe

Prolog
April 26, 1986

Olexsandr Diatlov walked past the security gate for Reactor 4. He'd left the university in Kiev only last week. Times were hard and his mother needed him. University would have to wait.

Olexsandr didn't mind. His mother rented a flat in the town of Pripyat near the river where fishing was good. The May holidays were coming. He would have time to fish and relax. Until then he had a job, and not a bad one. His uncle arranged the assignment. Not on the books, of course. Officially Olexsandr didn't work there. But his uncle managed the petty cash and no one asked questions. After all, jobs were hard to come by and Uncle Diatlov was important.

Olexsandr walked the perimeter fence, enjoying the fresh air. He wouldn't admit to anyone that life in Kiev wasn't as glamorous as everyone suggested. The longer he was in the city, the more he wanted to come home and walk the cart tracks that crossed the Ukrainian countryside linking one farm to another.

He shifted the rifle to the other shoulder. The weapon only came with one round. The USSR allocated resources carefully.

Uncle Diatlov didn't normally work night shift, but he was there now in the bowels of the great facility. He'd mumbled something about a routine test.

An owl called to Olexsandr beyond the fence. He turned his back to the facility lights and scanned the woods watching his breath push through the chain link. The owl's sound floated through darkness.

Olexsandr's shadow flashed long across the field beyond the fence. A burst of light illuminated the woods. In that instant, Olexsandr saw the owl. It was as if the creature had been watching for him, too. She stared, blinking, at the orange light emanating from the reactor. Olexsandr turned to see it.

The fire brought welcome warmth to the air around him as three thousand tons of radio-active graphite erupted from Chernobyl's Power Complex. Olexsandr squinted at the surreal heat, temporarily blinded.

Chunks of phosphorescing metal spat from Reactor 4, igniting fires in the forests around Pripyat. One fiery piece expelled by the blast superheated as it flew, combustion feeding off the oxygen streaming past.

Olexandr saw it coming, but didn't know what it was. He blinked at the spark, trying to remove the spot on his retina. Surely that's what it was. When it hit him, the shard burned its way through his middle, leaving a cauterized hole large enough for a man's hand.

The grass behind him was on fire before Olexandr hit the ground.

Chapter 1
Morris, Pennsylvania

The biological lab of Evans, Matthew and Fein maintained a remarkably unpretentious exterior. Apart from the chain-link fence, the low industrial building with a brown metal roof gave no indication of its real operation.

Aside from those employees who worked there under strict confidentiality agreements, few people knew the lab extended a full five floors beneath the main. The research facility produced flu vaccines on the first floors, and darker creations on the floors below. Biological labs receive a hazard rating of one through four based on the potential danger and level of risk. Hazard Level 4 labs are for fatal viruses and bacteria for which there is no known treatment or vaccine.

Evans, Matthew and Fein Level 4 bio containment facility, located five floors below the main, was affectionately called 'Fifth Lab.' Operating under tightly controlled government oversight, they fulfilled contracts to supply various civilian and government research labs with highly contagious pathogens for further study.

With 50,000 square feet of space, the scientists on the fifth sub floor grew the largest variety of Hazard Level 4 pestilence in the United States. Myriad tendrils of coiled ventilation hoses hung above the self-contained work floor. Every scientist working in the facility had to complete full suit training before being allowed to set foot in Fifth Lab.

Shipments of live virus traveled to and from the facility in compliance with strict guidelines developed by the Department of Transportation and the International Air Transportation Authority. All biological samples were packaged, shipped and transported by authorized couriers.

Due to the nature of the work, most scientists employed in the lab had military background or were civilians with high level security clearances. The lab's computer network functioned entirely off grid and operated with a two-tiered energy back-up system and state of the art critical redundancy to bring the danger as close to zero as possible, while still turning a profit.

The computerized security and containment systems had been methodically installed and inspected by Preston Farwick.

He completed that job a year ago; three days before he was fired.

Chapter 2
March 12

She used a black pen. Black ink on cream paper. Tape held the card in the center of the bathroom mirror. She hadn't even bothered to use an envelope. It clung there like a love note or grocery list or a reminder to take out the trash.

Preston Farwick fingered it off, heard the kissing noise of tape pulling away from its spot on the mirror, and held it up to the light.

Only two words.

I'm leaving.

Chapter 3
March 19

Spring rains mired Pennsylvania fields. Farmers had to leave their tractors stuck in caking, brown mud.

Pastor Philip Blithe looked out the window of his church office at the fields one block over. Rain and spring came simultaneously. Uncut grass grew irreverently across his property. Maintenance crews, like everyone else, were waiting for the rain to stop.

His own life sank into a different field. Six months ago, Lisa—his Lisa—took her life. The horror of that still woke him up and set him pacing the house.

Philip sighed and dropped the curtain back into place. His electric heater grumbled out a white noise that didn't cover the barrage of recriminations hounding him. At times it got so bad he walked into the sanctuary and lay on the altar. He'd never been that desperate before. Not about anything.

He knew it was too much for him. It was the kind of storm that could turn a man bitter. He had no choice but to lay there weeping and, with nothing else to say, hope the God he talked so much about would lift the heavy stone off his chest so he could take another breath and go on living.

Elizabeth and Ashley needed him. If it weren't for them, then maybe he too...

Philip shook his head and stared at the blank legal pad. His sermons had grown shorter. Most Sundays he would pull an old prayer book and pick a homily to read. Words.

His wife, Elizabeth, oddly, seemed to be doing well. Where before she had been buried in fear and depression, Lisa's death somehow re-calibrated her mind. For Ashley, it was different. When his daughter was able to get out of bed, he could tell she went through her days pushing back against the memories with a focus and academic drive she'd never had.

But he wasn't blind. At least, he was trying to be less blind. Lisa had fallen into the oblivion of self-hatred while he preached and mentored and managed the church. He wouldn't let Ashley go the same way.

Philip pressed fingers into his eyes, tried to remember what he said the few times parishioners faced the death of a loved one. "Time will heal."

It was poppycock. He knew that now. Time just extends the duration of one's suffering. Pain only heals as others pour in unexpected kindness. His wife. A trusted friend. Even Jesus.

But Philip wondered that Jesus got the worst of it. When sadness wasn't pressing the air from his lungs, Philip would stand at the church podium, face the cross on the back wall beyond the choir loft and tell Jesus how he got this all wrong.

A knock brought Philip back to the moment.

He pulled open the door. Chase Hikeman stared back at him through thick glasses. The boy had a weedy unprotected look about him.

Philip stood aside to let him into his office. "Come in."

Chase nodded, but didn't move. He'd never been into the inner sanctum of the church before. Thick theological books with gold leaf lettering on canvas spines stood at attention on the shelves.

"Is there a problem?" Philip asked.

"Well, I guess I kind of expected to find God hanging out in here with you." The boy stared at the heavy chestnut beams of the vestry's vaulted ceiling.

"Ashley told me you didn't believe in God," Philip said.

"I don't. But it doesn't hurt to be careful."

"No. I suppose it doesn't," Philip chuckled.

Chase squinted at the books, looking remarkably comfortable in the man's office. Maybe, thought Philip, he was just comfortable with himself.

He realized he knew almost nothing about this boy. Chase Hikeman's hair did what it liked and the boy's glasses hid what were otherwise bright snappy eyes. "You like to read?" Philip asked.

"Yes, but I haven't read much theology."

"What then?"

"Right now I'm reading a book by Bernard Heuvelman about creatures unknown to science. He's a French zoologist, but it's translated into English."

"I see." Philip didn't know what to make of the teenager, so he changed the subject. "Thanks for coming. I hope you can help."

"What do you mean?"

"It's Ashley," he said. "She's not doing well. For a while we thought she was getting better, but now…" Philip perched on the edge of his desk and scratched his neck.

Chase stared at the floor, suddenly shy. "Why did you call me?"

"Because you're the only true friend she has."

"I doubt that," Chase demurred. "She's got lots of friends."

"That's not what she told me," Philip replied.

Chase stared at him, genuinely surprised. "No kidding," he whispered.

Philip continued. "Ashley's school's been calling. She hasn't gotten out of bed in days. I was hoping a friend might help where I've failed."

Chase looked up at the stained glass window floating above the man's desk. "Okay. I guess I'll have to think up a reason to get her out of bed."

Chapter 4
March 20

Chase Hikeman met Ralph in the reading room of the public library.

Ralph traded in black nail polish for a garish lime green. He dressed like a confused Goth, but Chase didn't really care what he was. Ralph was the best computer hack he knew, and they were going to need him.

"I have another plan," Chase said.

"Good. Your last one sucked." The chain dangling from Ralph's pocket scraped the wooden chair as he sat.

"Thanks for that," Chase grimaced. "This one is going to work."

"Hit me," Ralph said. "I'm game."

"Okay. We need to get closer to The Moderator."

"How?" Ralph asked.

"We're going to play the game."

Ralph laughed. "You are out of your freaking mind."

"Probably."

"We can't do that. It's a small miracle we weren't hauled in before. Hacking into the juvenile justice data files didn't exactly set the right tone for future detective work. If we play the game, we're going to end up doing more illegal stuff."

"I know." Chase replied.

Ralph stared at him and shrugged. "Okay. So long as you know that. How are we going to make it work?"

"We need to create a player loop."

"Cool." Ralph lowered his voice. "What the hell is that?"

Chapter 5
March 21

Her dad said he could go on in, but it felt strange. Chase pushed open the front door. He expected the home to feel like the inside of the church. It was the rectory, after all.

Ashley hated when he called it that, said it reminded her of 'rectum.' But he'd never been inside. They usually met on the porch or at the park.

The kitchen was smaller than he anticipated. It was clean and the house didn't smell like cigarette smoke. Not that he paid much attention to that smell in his own house, but he noticed when it wasn't there.

"Hello?" Chase didn't want to surprise anyone. No answer. Her mother must be out.

Following directions, he went upstairs. Ashley's door stood open.

At first he thought her bed was empty. The covers heaped up in a tangled mess around the middle. Nothing moved. But blond hair lay across a crumpled pillow. She was still in bed. Just like her dad said.

Chase took a breath. He'd never really thought Ashley might like him. Might actually call him a friend. She followed him occasionally on crazy explorations around town, but he figured it had only been because she was curious.

You're the only true friend she has. That's what her dad said. Chase figured he wasn't lying. Pastors probably didn't lie, especially with God watching all the time like that.

But she didn't *act* like she liked him very much. He wasn't good with girls. In fact, he really didn't talk to any except Ashley.

The room smelled like her. A dusty ceiling fan hung above the bed. Her school backpack slumped in the corner, bored and tired looking. It was Saturday.

He could feel the sadness here. A picture of Lisa on a wardrobe was the only decoration. Torn triangles of paper still clinging to walls marked where posters had once hung. He guessed they came down after the suicide. Funny what doesn't matter when someone dies.

Of course, he'd thought about death. Who wouldn't? Most people got sad when they thought about it. It made him want to get on with living. After all, as far as he could tell, this was all there was.

Her uniform tartan skirt and a white polo shirt hung over the back of her desk chair. He picked them up and folded them. Shoes lay scattered about the floor. He rummaged around until he found matching pairs and lined them up under her bed.

Two towering pin oak trees dominated the view from her window. A bundle of leaves showed where a squirrel nested. Chase liked squirrels. They were smart and determined and happy.

Ashley didn't stir. He could see her hair and a few freckles on the side of her face. Covers buried the rest of her. Maybe he wouldn't have felt awkward if she wasn't so hot. He couldn't help noticing that. She even smelled pretty.

Now he didn't know what to do.

He cleared his throat. "I guess you can't go out like that," he said finally.

Her breathing changed. She heard him.

"I know. What am I doing in your bedroom, right?" Chase asked the obvious. He shrugged and sat down next to the snarl of blankets. "I have no idea," he answered his own question.

Her muffled voice emerged from the covers. "Go away."

"I was thinking of that, but I'm on assignment, you know."

She didn't respond.

"Your dad told me to ask you out." He paused. "Okay, that wasn't exactly how he put it."

He looked over at the pile that was her. "You can kill him later. Right now you need to get your ass out of bed."

"Why?" It was a whisper.

Chase wasn't sure how to answer that. He thought for a minute. Watched the black second hand of the wall clock take its slow walk the whole way 'round before answering. "Well, I guess because you're making me sad." The words tightened up in his throat. He hadn't expected that. "It's like," he fought back the lump, "it's like you've stopped living."

She didn't move. "And when you do that," he said, "one of my favorite parts of life stops living too."

A warm wet thing ran down his face, surprising him. She stirred and peeked out. He pulled off his glasses and mashed the tears away.

"If you want to stop living like this, then all I can do is bring you flowers. Like I do for Lisa." Chase pushed on. "Besides, I need your help."

"What for?" The whisper again.

"To find the asshole."

"What asshole?" she asked.

"The Moderator. I have a plan."

The bundle of covers moved and Ashley's face appeared. "This going to be better than your last idea?"

"Probably not. But I'm hoping it will get you out of bed."

"You're a turd."

"Yes. And this turd is going to sit here until you give me an answer."

"Go away. I have to get dressed."

Chapter 6

April 3

The department secretary tacked the memorandum on the cork bulletin next to the DARE school schedule and the FBI's Most Wanted notices.

TO: Law Enforcement Agencies in Lancaster, York and Dauphin Counties.
FROM: Excelsior Energy
SUBJECT: Three Mile Island Emergency Warning Systems Refit

The Island has solicited contractor proposals for the refit and replacement of all warning sirens within a ten mile radius of its nuclear facility. Refits will be conducted over a period of three weeks. No interruption of emergency warning service is expected.

Chapter 7
April 3

"So what motivates a guy like that?" Officer Dixon straddled a chair in Preston Farwick's office. They'd spend the morning speculating on the data files Dixon received from local kids who hacked into the Juvenile Justice system. They pulled records for other kids who got into trouble playing a computer game run by someone they called 'The Moderator.'

"Motivation?" Farwick asked.

"Yes. Why does he do it? I mean this guy doesn't appear to be a sexual pervert—at least not that we can tell. What's he after?"

Dixon was frustrated. Those who played had been blackmailed, others played along because they were already angry, disillusioned or bored. He didn't like cleaning up after The Moderator made a mess of their lives. But there was no one to arrest. The kids all checked out. Every one of them received the invitation to play from another kid. But there were too many broken links in the chain to take them back to ground zero.

Farwick closed the last of the folders and slid it into the accordion file. "Power."

"What do you mean?"

"I think he plays because he likes to feel powerful. That's why kids play video games with an avatar. They can do and say and play things they'd never try in real life. This guy has taken it to the obvious next level. Now he uses the players as his own avatars. You have to admit, it's clever."

Dixon shook his head. "When I was a kid, Pac-Man was clever. This is a *long* way from Pac-Man. But what kind of person wants to make his virtual world the reality?"

"Maybe he used to be powerful and something happened. Maybe his wife left him or he lost his job or he's working where no one appreciates him. Maybe he was bullied as a kid and has now found a way to feel powerful."

"Come on. Every kid gets bullied here and there. Even me. Face it, with a name like Dixon. Grade school boys don't care how it's spelled, but they know how it sounds." Dixon spread his arms. "But look at me. I turned out to be a reasonably well adjusted pain-in-the-ass."

Farwick laughed. "You can afford to act well-adjusted. You get to carry a weapon around and shoot the people who piss you off."

"Only if they start it," Dixon countered.

"Don't you see? You've grown up to find your own way to feel powerful and in control," Farwick paused. "Not everyone finds it in the same way."

"Now you sound like a shrink," Dixon said. "So how do we catch him?"

"I don't know. This guy is invisible."

Dixon grabbed his empty mug and stood. "Damn it."

He walked out. Farwick locked his fingers behind his head and spoke to the closed door. "You won't ever catch him."

Chapter 8
April 4

The door stood closed. Shafts of light fingered their way underneath. Chase crouched in the dark, ear pressed against the cold wood, feeling the man standing beyond, hidden in the hallway. The man was smiling. He was never sure how he knew that, but dreams are funny that way.

And Chase would wait, listening. At first he would only hear breathing. Nothing sick, just normal breathing. He could hear the brush of the man's clothing. Keys jingled faintly in a pocket. Outside of this dream, maybe from another dream, Ashley called.

Always it was the same. Then the man said his name. Every time Chase would take out a paper and pencil, copy the name down and put it back in the drawer of his night stand. He knew he could go back to sleep now that he finally knew the name. In the morning, he would take it to the police.

They would catch The Moderator. The man who stole the life out of Lisa. The man who manipulated Ashley with fear and shame.

Then he *would* wake up. His penlight flicked on. Finnicky would stir at his feet, but the Jack Russell didn't get up. Every time Chase opened the dresser drawer, rummaged frantically for the note pad. The white eye of light would scan the page.

Nothing.

No name. Just a dream.

Chapter 9
April 5

The symbol pulsed over a yellow background.   Black triangles spreading from point zero. The black hole. The unlucky clover. Radioactive.

The Moderator touched the screen with his fingers, thinking.

A symbol for world domination. A symbol of fear.   For him, it meant absolute power.

He managed a small army of players who would do anything he asked. They owed him. They feared him. There were too many to track now. Too many to keep tabs on. But it always surprised him how willing players were to participate, even when he didn't have any kind of leverage. "What is this world coming to?" he wondered.

He would make his biggest move.

His old employer, Evans, Matthew & Fein would have no choice. They were about to be played by the nuclear reactor a few miles upriver. He would plunge the bio-research lab into a kind of chaos for which they had no contingency plan.

Of course they would never know it was him. He would never get the credit. But *he* would know.

It was payback time.

Chapter 10
April 7

I know. The Moderator was online. The reply appeared impassively before the player.

The cursor blinked in open space.

RUSH typed: *You know what?*

You have AIDS. The three words stared from the screen like malignancies on an x-ray.

Blackmail. Hands hovered over plastic keyboard. RUSH balled hands into fists. The Moderator was waiting.

Nothing. Silent fingers. RUSH stared. Watching. Holding his breath. Finally fists unfurled like a wet flag. Cold fingers worked the keys. Deliberate. One word. Then another.

What do you want?

RUSH's index finger touched Enter. Pushed down. The words disappeared.

More waiting. RUSH shifted into the lotus, toes pulled high onto his thighs. Straight back. Breathe in. Center. Breathe out.

New words materialized. The Moderator replied: *I thought you'd never ask.*

Chapter 11
April 8

Chester Brightman parked the truck behind the tennis courts and turned off the diesel.

The Terex Hi-Ranger bucket truck boasted a working height of sixty feet. The telephone pole rose an easy forty. He walked to the rear of the truck and pushed in the security key to activate hydraulic power. A light flashed as dual outriggers whined into place, leveling the truck against the swale built to keep water off the courts. They were empty now. Spring or not, the air was too damn cold for anyone but hard core players.

The orange indicator blinked green and the outriggers stopped when the sensor indicated level. He returned to the truck, grabbed a pair of gloves from behind the seat and picked up his travel mug.

The boom folded in half over the truck bed. Brightman fastened on a tool belt from one of the white aluminum tool cabinets.

ACS T-128's sirens were substantially smaller than their predecessors but still cumbersome. Each unit weighed a hair under seventy pounds. Brightman unclipped the wire lock pin and slid the square-channel arm from the side of the bucket. It would support the 128's weight until he bolted it into place. But first he had to remove the relic.

He climbed into the bucket, clipped his safety harness in place and put a hand on the control. The hydraulic motor whined as the boom rose from its nest toward the old siren mounted on the pole overhead. The Cyclone was a forty horsepower unit with a sound output of 120 decibels at one hundred yards, thirty two times louder than seventy decibels. Ear drums rupture at 150 decibels. Brightman dropped ear protection over his head. There weren't any emergency siren tests scheduled. Still, no need to take chances.

The come-along reel complained as he played out the cable far enough to clip the locking carabiner into place on the unit's lift ring. The anchor bolts came loose, and the hydraulics whined again as he lowered the Cyclone back to earth, officially retiring it. He'd sell it on eBay and make a little extra money. Not that he needed it; this job alone would pay for his truck.

Chapter 12
April 10

RUSH pushed off from a run-down river marina four hundred meters north of the barrier island and upstream of the reactor. The facility's four cooling towers rose up against grey sky. He steered the borrowed duck boat toward shore. Sand and rock scraped underneath green aluminum, and RUSH clambered out. It would have been easier to come in from the road running parallel to the river, but this was safer.

A fishing rod and tackle box lay unused on the floor of the boat. RUSH had forgotten the worms. It would be hard to convince anyone the purpose of the trip was fishing without worms.

Better not to get stopped at all. RUSH dragged the boat further on shore and glanced around before wading into the woods sandwiched between the river and the road. A rail-spur split off to service the reactor compound. RUSH skipped across the graveled rail line and stopped on the berm beside the road. He removed the camouflaged, hunters' camera from a pack and oriented it to capture traffic departing from the facility. Nothing illegal. Not yet.

The motion-activated camera would only stay in place twenty-four hours. The Moderator wanted pictures.

Chapter 13
April 11

Preston Farwick watched the picture file transfer across the secure router to his hard drive.

Cookie scratched at the door. Farwick wasn't sure why he'd shut the door. There was no danger of his wife coming in. Not anymore.

The dog carried a tattered tennis ball in her mouth and climbed onto the office sofa. Cookie dropped the ball from her mouth and watched it roll across the floor. She got down, picked up the ball and dropped it in Farwick's lap.

"Not now, Cookie. I'm working." Farwick lifted the slobbery ball from his lap and tossed it. Cookie came to life, toenails scratching the floor as she chased the ball, crashing between the trash can and the desk.

"Cookie," Farwick grumbled. "Go to bed."

The German shepherd slinked toward the sofa and climbed back on, to sulk with the broken ball in her mouth.

Farwick flicked through the folder. The motion-activated camera worked better than he had hoped. Every single vehicle leaving the facility in a twenty-four hour period had been captured on film. The resolution wasn't great, but he could make out license plate numbers.

He breezed through the pictures. "Let's see," he said to himself. Then he stopped. "Bingo." Farwick said. "I've got one."

A red pick-up truck. Just what he needed.

"Do you know what that is, Cookie?"

The dog lifted her head.

"This, my dear friend, is a way in. My transport vehicle."

Chapter 14
April 12

CRETAN got the shopping cart from hell. The front left wheel spun in useless circles and the back right tire had a flat spot which caught and dragged at every other turn. Username CRETAN walked down the aisle of the hardware store, glad at least for the humor of the farting noises the flat wheel made when it stopped turning. He fought the recalcitrant cart around a corner under a banner reading 'Lawn and Garden.'

A store clerk teetered on a ladder, picking at the plastic wrap around a pallet load of hummingbird lawn ornaments.

"Can I help you?" The clerk eyed him suspiciously. CRETAN didn't exactly look like a green-thumb.

"Yes, my mom said I'm supposed to pick up a large bag of fertilizer."

"Did she say what kind she needed?"

CRETAN made a face as if trying to remember. "She called it pot ash in salt paste, I think."

The clerk laughed. "I think you mean 'potassium sulfate.'"

CRETAN shrugged. "Whatever. Anyway, I need to get a big bag."

The clerk descended the ladder and pointed to the end of the aisle. "It's right down there. We've got ten, twenty and fifty pound bags. Take your pick."

"Thanks." CRETAN flashed the peace sign complete with two green-painted fingernails and pretended not to notice her eyes roll.

He pushed the farting cart past the ladder to the bags. Looks like cocaine, he thought. I wonder what he wants with this?

Chapter 15
April 13

The two water towers held more than 200,000 gallons of water overhead. But CLINGER wasn't interested in water. Or more precisely, The Moderator wasn't interested in water. CLINGER stared up at a caged-in, metal ladder welded to the outside of the tower. Not today. That would come later, she knew.

She'd already charged the drone's batteries and installed the app on her phone. CLINGER set the drone on the grass and continued down the sidewalk. After rechecking the area, she opened the control app. The drone had three cameras, one mounted on the nose, two beneath. She selected the nose camera and lifted off. The neighborhood spun across the view screen. She corrected the drone's direction, navigating in low over the grass before ascending up around the water tower. She'd spent hours practicing with the drone around her house when no one was home. This was different. The breeze made it harder, but the view streamed to her phone was breathtaking. She felt the thrill of being able to see where others could not. The rush of watching the world, knowing the world couldn't see. When the drone neared the top, CLINGER clicked the red 'REC' button. The drone was now recording.

She resisted the desire to stare up at the helicopter. She'd taken the time to paint the drone swimming-pool blue in hopes of blending in against the sides of the massive tank. The drone spiraled around the tower and leveled off at the top.

A crow, perched on the catwalk railing, eyed the drone suspiciously and took off.

CLINGER navigated over the water tank, making sure the drone's camera's got good coverage. Antennae bristled from the tower and a strange cone-shaped hat sat squarely on the top center of the tank. CLINGER didn't know what it was, but it mattered to The Moderator.

The drone circled the cone. A metal plate riveted to its side appeared on the phone's screen. She moved the drone a little closer until the numbers on the plate came into focus. CLINGER spun the craft so the camera could record the serial numbers on the antennae bolted to the perimeter railing. The Moderator would like that.

Satisfied, CLINGER directed the drone away from the water tower and steered over the neighborhood. She navigated through the broken window of a decaying barn, found her mark and touched 'land.' The drone settled onto a broken wooden barrel, and the whirring blades fell silent.

Chapter 16

April 13

Preston Farwick selected the photograph, zoomed in and jotted the license plate number on a sticky note. Good, he thought.

He opened a browser, typed in *publicdata.com* and logged into an account registered to another 'user' who, of course, knew nothing about it.

"God bless America," he muttered. The Freedom of Information Act granted anyone access, albeit for a small fee, to the registry of license plate numbers.

Of course, he could have come up with a story and asked the Florin Police Department secretary to run the plate. This was easier. Farwick completed the request form and clicked submit. He'd have an address in twenty-four hours.

Chapter 17
April 13

Chase lived in a converted broom factory. The conversion may have added apartments but the building certainly hadn't shaken the factory look. Chase met Ralph on the sidewalk out front.

"Hey Ralph," Chase said.

"This place looks like the projects." Ralph stood staring at the tall, multi-paned windows.

"What do you know about the projects?" Chase asked.

"Everything there is to know from watching television."

"Great. What did you learn about The Moderator?" Chase avoided the comment. In truth, he hated his apartment. Hated the pervasive smell of smoke; hated the sound of mothers screaming at their kids, hated the scooters racing up and down the central hallway.

"That guy is the bomb," Ralph replied.

"What do you mean?" Chase asked.

"I wonder how many players he's got? It must be like having his own private company, but he doesn't pay anyone. He knows you'll do what you're told because he thinks you've got AIDS and don't want anyone to find out. He knows I'll do what he asks because I told him my mother does drugs and he thinks I'm afraid Children and Youth will take me away for it." Ralph stared up at the sky. "Why didn't I think of this?"

Chase scowled, "Because you're above using other people."

Ralph shook his head. "Right. It is kinda creepy."

"Kinda?" Chase prodded.

"Well, okay. Really creepy. But you have to admit the guy's a genius. Shit, he can do anything he wants. He'll keep getting more and more players until he can run the freaking world."

"Which is why we need to stop him."

"You're right. He's a shit-head, but he's a genius shit-head."

"Whatever, Ralph." Chase replied. "What did you learn?"

"I'm not sure. I bought the man—at least we think he's a man—a fifty pound bag of yard fertilizer. He even slipped me the cash. It was taped to the inside of a newspaper box right where he said it would be. The guy must be a garden fanatic."

"What kind of fertilizer?"

"Potassium sulfate," Ralph replied.

Chase pushed the glasses up on his nose and looked at Ralph. "I wonder what he's going to do with that?"

"Keep the weeds down?" Ralph suggested.

"Or make a bomb," Chase replied.

Ralph's eyes got big. "Dude! Could he?" he said.

Chapter 18
April 14

A boxer growled at the hedge, but Username R8R kept moving. This wasn't a normal run. The pickup and drop-off coordinates had been provided by The Moderator who insisted R8R complete this task at a specific time. But people usually don't go geocaching in neighborhoods. R8R paused, lifted the handheld GPS, and waited for it to secure another satellite. Perfect. Twelve of them.

He was getting close.

The tingle on R8R's spine warned him this might not be a good idea. There were all kinds of creeps in the world. He'd taken the precaution of slipping a fixed blade knife into his jeans in case he needed a little back-up.

Evening commuter traffic picked up as folks returned from work. It wasn't going to be as easy as he thought.

R8R glanced at the GPS. This was the place.

A derelict, single-carriage barn leaned up against the alley. The finder indicated he was just feet from the drop zone. R8R pressed his back to the barn. Dog piles sat in the yard dissolving slowly into the spring mud.

He ducked through the bottom half of a Dutch-style door and blinked in the dim light. Moving toward a narrow staircase he kicked into a galvanized watering can. The racket spooked a rabbit in its cage and R8R flew up the stairs to the haymow. The blue quad copter sat on a wooden barrel. The metal band on the bottom of the barrel was missing and the staves splayed out beneath it. The red LED light on the drone blinked intermittently.

R8R glanced out the carriage house window and froze. A woman hurried toward the barn. The door squeaked open. There was no way for him to hide.

"Excuse me. Can I help you?" She stared up at him suspiciously.

R8R looked down from the loft and forced a smile. "Hi. My helicopter landed in your barn."

She put her hands on her hips. He held out the drone, heart pounding in his neck as she studied him.

"That's a funny looking helicopter," she said. "Best you fly that in the park. You're liable to lose it on someone's roof."

Chapter 19
April 15

Preston Farwick drove the long way home. He needed to make a little detour. The dog would have to wait.

His players were doing well. A grand puzzle, falling together piece by piece.

Sunshine spilled through a break in the black front of clouds, a surreal brilliance after incessant rain. Rafts of seagulls floated over the fields, drawn inland where they could feast on grubs and worms that started moving with warmer weather. Farwick turned away from town and drove past the mill, cut across a single lane bridge and followed a fence line running along the road. A crumbling lime kiln squatted among a grove of scrub trees. Farwick checked his mirrors before turning onto a dirt track that cut around behind the kiln and out of view.

Farwick killed the engine and looked around. He had to be alone.

There were safer methods, but everything took time. He needed to jump up the pace of the operation. The spring air flicked up the collar of his coat and wet grass immediately soaked through his loafers. A stone foundation supported a large bowl lined with firebrick where limestone was once converted to powder for use as mortar or field fertilizer. Now a hundred years of leaves and brush all but hid the burn bowl.

Farwick stooped down and swept a few leaves away from the top of the kiln. An iron grate, probably installed to keep kids from playing in the kiln, kept larger branches from falling in. A car approached. He froze, waiting for it to pass by. The driver hadn't seen him. Farwick pushed a few branches aside, reached through the grate and felt among the leaves. His fingers found a plastic container. Working it through the eight inch gap between the bars, he tucked the container under his arm.

"Good boy, R8R. Good boy."

Back at home Preston Farwick opened the plastic container, removed the memory stick from the RC helicopter and plugged it into a USB port.

Farwick navigated to the root folder, opened the saved footage and clicked play.

The picture filled the screen. The quad copter rose steadily, spiraling around the water tower. CLINGER had obviously practiced. He paused the screen and studied the siren to scrutinize the antennae arrangement.

This might work, he thought.

Farwick pushed his keyboard out of the way and rolled out an area map. Red dots indicated every one of the sirens within a ten mile radius of the nuclear facility. The refit of the sirens was still underway, but soon all ninety-two of the Cyclones and Penetrators would be replaced by the new ACS T-128 sirens.

The new sirens were radio operated. Signals sent from each county's siren-control panel activated all the sirens in that county. After the upgrade, all sirens could be activated using a certain code-embedded frequency from a single radio transmission.

When the refit was done, Farwick would be ready.

Chapter 20
April 16

Username SAVAGE looked at the address on her hand and strolled down the sidewalk until she found the right number. The development had a sleepy Saturday morning feel. Every third house looked alike. Burgundy or green shutters on the same white siding. A few owners added a tree to the putting green lawn separating front doors from mail boxes. She double checked the number. This was it.

SAVAGE picked up the disposable camera at a pharmacy. The Moderator wanted prints. Go figure. Old school.

The porch on the house looked like an afterthought. A baby stroller leaned against the wall by the front door. A newer truck sat in the driveway. The garage was probably bursting with the clutter of life with little kids.

SAVAGE snapped pictures. Including one of the truck bed. The Moderator had been quite specific. Weird.

But SAVAGE wasn't about to argue. Give The Moderator what he wanted. She looked around, snapped the last few shots and tucked the camera into her windbreaker.

SAVAGE moved off. The photos needed to be developed and left at the drop site before six.

Chapter 21
April 17

Some days the depression pressed into bed like a thumbtack in wood. Other times, the haunting images of Lisa made Ashley rush into her day so she could get busy and forget them.

The sound of her name came from another world. It was her mother. Ashley didn't want to wake up, didn't want to face the real world.

She lay in the blissful numb of near sleep, trying to keep her brain from starting. Then the familiar dread surged, stealing away the warm blanket of ignorance. The memories came unbidden, like a television program someone else turns on. She saw again the blood-tainted saliva bubbling from her sister's lips, Lisa's face contorted in the agony of overdose.

Ashley leapt from bed, terror-driven to stop her mind. She pulled on jeans and socks and jacket with numb automaticity. She tried to focus on the pattern of her carpet. Anything to wash out the pictures.

Chase Hikeman was waiting when she came down stairs. He sat at the kitchen table, eating a bagel her mom had made for him.

"Hey," she said.

"Did you know that eating a bagel is the carbohydrate equivalent of five slices of bread?" Chase sucked jam off his lip before stuffing in the last mouthful.

She shrugged. She didn't give a damn and really wanted to say so, but her mom was in the kitchen. "I didn't know you were coming today." She gave her mom a look. Elizabeth shrugged. "Did Dad send you again?"

"Nope. I'm on auto-repeat now. Every Saturday morning. Rain or shine."

"Great." Her sarcasm didn't escape him. She noticed but kept going anyway, "Auto-repeat; like email spam."

Chase slouched a little in his chair. Wounded again.

Ashley shook her head. Angry at herself. Angry at her dad.

"Let's take a walk." She wanted to get out of the house anyway. Too many memories.

Chase thanked her mom for the food and they left.

The ground smelled wet and sweet and the sun shone warm for the first week of April. Chase didn't say much, and she didn't feel like talking. She'd been mean to him again. It made her miserable.

"I don't know why you keep coming over," Ashley said.

"Yes, you do."

She looked at him. Chase would probably always be small. He was strong in a wiry sort of way. He was like his dog, she decided. Strong, small, curious and determined to love you no matter what you did. She never had to wonder what he thought of her. Why she kept treating him like a dog was beyond her.

"I had the dream again," Chase said.

"Which one?"

"The one where The Moderator is standing on the other side of the door. He says his name, I write it down. Then I hear you calling, and I wake up. I keep expecting that one day I'll wake up and actually find a name written on my notepad."

"Weird," Ashley said. "How many times have you had the dream?"

"Ten, maybe more."

"Do you dream anything?" Chase asked.

"You mean about you?"

He blushed. "That's not what I meant."

"Not really. My bad dream happens when I wake up."

"You mean me?"

"No. I mean the memories." She stopped in a spot where a shaft of warm sunshine pushed through the trees. "I see her, Chase. Every morning I wake up to a sadness so heavy I can hardly breathe, or I see Lisa dying all over again. I see it: the seizure, the blood where her teeth clamped down on her tongue, the saliva bubbles…"

"What do you do to make it stop?"

"It never really stops. It's like this T.V. channel that's always playing. I can only turn on other stations in hopes of drowning the nightmare."

"I'm sorry," Chase said.

"No, Chase. I'm the one who's sorry. I keep treating you like shit, but you're the only one who ever listens to me. You're the only one who has the courage to come over and get me out of bed."

He pushed his hands deeper in his pockets. Chase looked down, shrugged and changed the subject. "Don't forget to meet me in the library this afternoon."

Chapter 22
April 17

Officer Ken Dixon stared at Chief Gregson. "I can't believe it."

"Believe it," the chief replied. "We've got no choice. The accountant says the money runs out after one year. End of discussion."

"Shit."

"Precisely." The chief sighed and rested his hands on his pot belly. "I like the guy, too. I know he's doing a great job at an impossible task, but there's nothing for it. Kramer's got the board by the short hairs, and he likes making other people dance."

"The board has no idea what we're dealing with," Dixon said. "One of these days they're gonna get burned by a bad guy. Then they'll get it."

"Fat chance. That happens and we'll still get the blame." Gregson made a face. "Kramer's a first-class, pompous, white-assed wind bag and honorary member of the good 'ol boys club. The best we can hope is that he'll have a massive coronary and retire early."

"I volunteer to buy him donuts."

Gregson snorted. "Not a bad idea, but it isn't going to work fast enough to save Preston's job."

"When are you going to tell him?" Dixon asked.

"Not sure. I want to give him time to look for another job," Gregson said.

"This is stupid." Dixon crossed his arms.

"Yes, it is."

"So much for 'Preserving the peace.'"

"Yep. Our job isn't about justice. It's a plastic-faced dance around small town politics."

"Shit." Dixon said again. "I hate politics."

Chapter 23

April 17

SAVAGE logged on, got the drop location from The Moderator and left home, walking quickly toward Main Street. Florin had been trying desperately to revitalize the down town area. Brick formed sidewalks and decorative planters replaced the cracked grey concrete. The town clock received a face lift and the few eateries managed to scrape along.

Higher Grounds Cafe was one of the few shops that thrived in a reclaimed row home. Purple walls and yellow trim popped on an otherwise dull block. Good coffee sold in real ceramic mugs juiced up those of the Florin workforce who might have stayed a little too long at area bars the night before. SAVAGE paid for a coffee with lots of room for cream.

She added three sugar packets and headed to the lounge in the back of the café. Halogen lights dangled from long lines over retro diner stools and tall tables. The wall murals competed with the dull spring and actually made her feel happy, if only for a moment.

The Moderator gave her the dead drop location after she picked up the pictures. He obviously didn't want to give her extra time.

In other circumstances, it might have been exciting. But not with The Moderator's reputation. She had no idea what he was up to, but she knew him well enough to know it wasn't good.

Play the game. Do it right. Give him what he wants.

SAVAGE set her coffee on a pedestal table. He might even be there. Watching her. No, she decided, he probably wouldn't risk it. Being invisible was all he had.

An older man packed up his newspaper and shuffled out. She gave her skinny jeans a hitch, slipped into the unisex restroom and locked the door, fighting back the sick feeling that threatened. What if he *was* watching her? A suspicious red LED glared back at her from a smoke detector, if that's what it really was. Anyone could get a spy-camera smoke detector online.

She ran a long black fingernail gently under the wig, trying to scratch without disturbing the hair. Her head itched terribly. With shaking fingers SAVAGE pulled the envelope of prints from her handbag, slipped them into the packing envelope and sealed the top.

The door rattled, and SAVAGE jumped. "Sorry. Busy," she called, trying to sound pleasant. SAVAGE cranked the window knob the wrong way and heard it pop. She whispered a curse and went the other way. Righty tighty, leftie loosey. It might help, she thought, if she remembered right and left when it really mattered. The window squeaked open. SAVAGE flushed the toilet behind her in hopes of covering the noise. Hurry up, she thought. Hurry.

The top-hinged window only opened an inch. She hoped it would be enough. The stiff envelope crinkled along the sides as she shoved it through to the window sill beyond. The Moderator would get his damn pictures, she thought. They might get wrinkles, but she'd get them through the window. The envelope caught on the brick outside but frantic fingers forced the last of it through before she squeaked the window shut again. Her chain belt snagged on the studded bracelet and she took a minute to untangle herself before leaving the bathroom.

The barista waved to her on the way out. He must like his girls punked out. She gave him a nod, but kept walking and left the coffee shop with an adrenaline buzz. Her coffee sat untouched on the back table. Oh well. It was time to get out of there. SAVAGE forced herself to walk.

It was all she could do not to turn around and look behind. The thought of being watched made her feel sick. At the end of the block, she turned and hurried towards the library.

#

Her heart thumped like a trapped bird. I wonder how Superman did it, she wondered. A bathroom stall was no place to change character. SAVAGE pulled a plastic bag from her handbag and hung it from the silver hook on the back of the door. The wig came off first. She gave her head a long scratch. I'd rather go bald, she thought. The wig felt awful. She twisted awkwardly in the confined space to peel off her jeans and pull on a pair of leggings. The thin cotton tunic went over top. It wrinkled badly in the plastic bag, but it couldn't be helped.

A deep breath helped a little. It had come off okay. SAVAGE tied the bag tight, forcing out the air and opened the stall door. A pink beanie settled her blond hair. Of course, she had no idea if he followed her. She only hoped he wanted the pictures more than he wanted to follow her, and he couldn't be in two places at once. What he wanted with pictures of a red pick-up truck made no sense.

SAVAGE left the bathroom and passed a few people working at computer stations. Shelves of DVDs and stacks of novels made a hallway leading back to the reading area. She grabbed a magazine from the rack, settled into one of three oak tables and listened to a patron browsing the novels behind her. Their feet moved closer. Then she remembered the black nails. Dropping her hands into her lap, she picked feverishly at the fake nails, pulled off the acrylic stickers and stuffed them into the outside pocket of her bag.

A hand touched her shoulder. SAVAGE stifled a shriek and jerked around.

"Hey, Ashley." It was Chase.

"You scared the shit out of me," she whispered.

"Sorry. How did it go?" he asked.

"Okay. I'm still jumpy."

"I noticed."

"Did you get the camera?" she asked.

"No. I didn't want to risk him seeing me," Chase said. "I'll get it later."

"Did you see anything?"

"Not really. Several people walked down the alley. It could have been any of them. I had no way of knowing who picked up the envelope, if he even came."

"How do we know it's a 'he'?" Ashley asked.

"Do you think it's a woman?"

"Well, no," she said.

"There you go then."

"What do you mean?"

"Women's intuition. Studies put the reliability rating of women's intuition at around eighty-five percent," Chase said.

"You made that up." Ashley gave him a sneer.

"How did you know?"

"Because you do a funny thing with your nose when you lie."

Chase grinned. "Guilty. Anyway, I did see several people. Mostly dog walkers, runners, and such."

"Any of them look like The Moderator," she asked.

"How would I know? No one's seen him."

"I dunno." Ashley shrugged. "I guess I expected him to look evil or guilty or something."

"The funny thing about real-life bad guys is they don't look like bad guys," Chase said. "Hopefully, the hunter's camera will give us what we want. I managed to get it into position in time, but it wasn't a great spot."

"What do you think he's after, Chase? How do we know when we've gone too far?"

Chase pulled off his glasses and stared at her. "I don't know, but I've got a bad feeling about it."

She leaned her head to the side. "And what's the reliability rating of your feeling?"

"That depends."

"On what?" she asked.

"If this guy is as bad as we think he is, I'd say it's pretty reliable."

Chapter 24
April 17

Preston Farwick tore open the envelope and spread the photographs of the red truck over his desk. A low profile diamond-plate aluminum tool box sat behind the cab.

He picked up a magnifying glass and studied the tool box design. The locking box rested on the sides, suspended 10 inches above the floor of the truck bed. Enough space for what he needed.

Farwick made a few notes and flicked off the desk light. "Come on, Cookie. Let's mix up a cocktail."

The dog followed Farwick downstairs to a partially finished basement. Florescent tube lights buzzed overhead. Cookie settled herself in the corner to watch.

The sound of Chopin filtered down from speakers upstairs. Farwick tied on a grimy shop apron. The workbench stretched a full eight feet against the wall. He flicked on a bench light and settled himself on a stool. He thumbtacked a handwritten recipe card above the work bench before switching on an electric hotplate.

A one gallon plastic bucket sat on a lab scale and Farwick set the tare weight before adding his first ingredient. Using a utility knife, Farwick sliced open the fifty pound bag of potassium sulfate. He scooped out a measuring-cup full and poured it into the bowl, watching the digital numbers rise. After seven cups of potassium sulfate he shook in a few more granules until the scale reached the magic number. He poured this into a stock pot and returned the plastic container to the scale.

"Now for the sweetener." Farwick ran a finger across the recipe card, double checking the amount. He measured the sugar and added it to the potassium sulfate.

Farwick spread a piece of wax paper over the work bench and set up a cheese grater. Then he pulled a block of paraffin wax from its box and started grating. When he had a pile, he moved it onto the scale and added a pinch more.

Farwick set the stock pot on the hot plate and watched the wax begin to melt. He mixed the slurry thoroughly, then poured the mixture into twelve cardboard tubes, tamped it down and pressed a pen into the top before it hardened to make space for the igniters.

The smoke bombs would have plenty of time to cool.

Chapter 25
April 17

The alley behind the café ran parallel to the train tracks. Chase Hikeman walked past the dead-drop location after dark. The envelope was gone. The sky had dried out and the wind felt warmer than he expected. A car with one headlight entered the alley and Chase shielded his face against the glare of the remaining bulb. He waited until the car turned at the end of the street before he walked back the way he came.

This might be it, he thought. For too long they'd been trying to figure out how to catch The Moderator. When their last attempt failed, Chase knew there was only one more option.

Play the game. Let The Moderator think they were new players. Create a player loop. It took some talking to convince Ashley, but he needed another player. Not that he minded having another reason to see her.

Ashley hadn't been the same since Lisa died. She was meaner and more sarcastic and didn't seem to care about anything. One day she worked like she was running out of time; the next she couldn't get out of bed.

He loved her anyway. She knew it, of course. Or tolerated it. He wasn't sure. At least she hadn't written him off, but he wondered if he could stand being 'only friends' for one more day. It might be easier if he stopped pretending she might fall in love with him. But he couldn't help himself.

Fat chance. She was trim, blond and drop-dead gorgeous. He knew he wasn't love blind. He'd seen the way other guys looked at her. Chase could almost read their mind; could almost hear them thinking, 'Why in the hell is she hanging out with that dweeb?'

He winced at the noise of gravel crunching underfoot. He ducked under the wooden staircase to a second floor apartment a few doors from the café. It was his best hope of getting pictures without getting caught. If he had more time, he might have found a better spot to put the camera, but Ashley hadn't been told where she was to drop the pictures until the last minute.

Chase felt along the four-by-four post for the camera. Nothing. He must be in the wrong place, but he didn't dare turn on his light and risk exposing himself. A couple argued upstairs. An all-too-familiar sound. Chase tried to ignore it and slid his fingers down another post. A splinter slid deep into his hand. He ground his teeth together and picked it out. Part of it stayed behind. The shouting grew louder upstairs and the apartment door opened; light spilled into the alley. Chase crouched low, hoping no one would come down the stairs. The woman yelled at her boyfriend. Called him interesting names. Told him he was a jealous, paranoid SOB and he could find another place to sleep.

The man stormed out, untied boots hammering on the stairs. He stopped half way down and turned, "Look, I didn't put it there," he protested.

"Like hell you didn't." She slammed the door. The argument ended and the boyfriend ran the rest of the way down the stairs. Chase pulled a hood over his head and buried his face against the wall, trying to be invisible. The man stalked off and Chase relaxed. He decided to hazard using his penlight. The narrow light flicked on and scanned the post where he'd put the camera.

Chase froze. It was gone. His mind started racing. The Moderator found it. Maybe he'd seen Chase put it there.

Chase darted back into the alley and walked away. Maybe The Moderator was still watching. Chase started running. He dodged a rain puddle and tried to think. Chase rounded a corner and kept moving. If The Moderator knew about him, he probably knew about Ashley, too. Panic started to jumble his mind. I have to get a grip, he thought.

He forced himself to stop running and take three full breaths. He wanted to call Ashley, to see if she was okay, but he didn't own a phone. His mom couldn't afford it and, aside from Ashley and Ralph, he didn't have anyone to call anyway.

His feet started moving toward her house. It would take more than ten minutes to walk there. Chase slipped into a trot. The thought that The Moderator might know about her made him move faster.

Then another thought wormed its way into Chase's mind. It rattled around for a full minute before Chase stopped running. Again he replayed the argument at the apartment.

Chase groaned. That woman had his camera.

Chapter 26
April 19

Chester Brightman took his breaks forty feet up. When he worked as a lineman for the phone company, this would never have been allowed. But hell, he owned the truck and the view was better up here.

A yellow-throated warbler flitted among the top branches of a tree, watching him. Brightman sat on a milk crate in the work bucket and sipped his coffee. The spring sun warmed his face and he unzipped his jacket.

Right out of high school he worked in a print shop. Regular hours, heavy lifting. Perfect for a kid who didn't know what he wanted to be when he grew up. Chester Brightman decided quickly that wasn't it. He couldn't stand being indoors.

He wondered how he survived high school. Window seats probably, he mused. That was nothing like this. He sighed happily. Not only did he have the best view around, he didn't have anybody breathing down his neck. The beauty of being self-employed.

The worst of it was the cold. Maybe he'd take his truck and move south to a place where they didn't believe in snow. But Excelsior Energy practically handed him their Federal Grant check to upgrade the emergency warning system. The new radio-activated sirens even used battery back-up systems. It was perfect. Back-up batteries had a shelf life. When the batteries needed to be replaced, he would be ready. He would finish refitting the last of the sirens by the week's end. Five sirens every day for almost four weeks. Long days. Lots of cash.

Brightman did the math again. He knew how it worked out, but it made him happy. He didn't want to think about the pound of flesh the Federal Government would steal in taxes, but he'd made more money in the last four weeks than in the last three years combined. Why had it taken him so long to leave the world of wage-labor?

He knew the answer: Company benefits.

Brightman allowed himself a chuckle. The golden handcuffs. It made sense. A man shackles himself to a job he hates, working for people he can't stand just so he can keep his benefits. Never mind the benefit of waking up in the morning without a sense of dread. Never mind the benefit of not experiencing that Sunday afternoon depression before another week hits.

He shook his head. No thanks. Even if he hadn't landed this contract and was still in debt up to his ears, this was way more fun. Good coffee, good views, plenty of cash and a portable business.

The warbler disappeared. Brightman drained the last of his coffee and wondered if there was bucket-truck work in the Caribbean.

Chapter 27
April 19

On days like this, Chief Gregson hated his job.

He wanted to fire off a hot email to Kramer and the rest of the board and tell them exactly where he thought they should put their budget, but they managed his salary and all the little line items he needed them to approve so the department could keep moving. So he'd smile, play along with their little power games and pretend to be grateful.

It was a bitter pill, but there was nothing for it, and he didn't want to wait any longer.

He grabbed his phone and rang Preston's four-digit extension.

Farwick picked up on the second ring.

"Farwick, stop by my office, would you?"

Three minutes later, Farwick came in. "Sir?"

"Come in. Sit down. I've got bad news." Gregson pushed on. He didn't believe in small-talk. "It's been great having your expertise here. But you're fighting cyber-crime—an invisible enemy. The guys with the real power are more concerned about the drop in revenue from parking tickets."

Farwick sat opposite Gregson's desk. "This doesn't sound good."

"No. I'm afraid it's not. I want to keep you around. Hell, we all do." Gregson waved the fourteen-page, budget packet and threw it back on his desk. "The board has not approved a continuation for your salary. I'm afraid one year is all we can give you."

Farwick leaned forward and held his head.

"You've got some time left, but I wanted to give you as much warning as possible. I know the job market isn't easy out there."

Farwick nodded.

Gregson made a face. "I wish I could help."

Chapter 28
April 21

A gauze-like cloud covered the moon. She wasn't sure why she was here. It didn't make sense. She didn't even know what was in the plastic box in her pack. As promised, the padlock on the gate had been cut. She pulled the last of the chain out, cringing at the rattle. The gate squeaked closed behind her. An open gate would be easy to spot.

It bothered her that she didn't know what she was doing, but maybe it was better that way. The Moderator sent her the package. The Moderator told her where to put it.

She touched the cold leg of the water tower. A single ladder ran up to a catwalk circling the girth of the tank. A second connected the catwalk with the top. A metal cage enclosed the first ladder, but the first ten feet didn't exist. A safety consideration.

CLINGER pulled on her climbing shoes and powdered her fingers. A rope ladder had been attached beneath, giving her access. She wondered who put it there. Doubtless another gamer. She wondered how many players worked for The Moderator.

It was like a huge puzzle, and she only had a few pieces.

The rope ladder kicked out under her weight. It wasn't attached at the ground and CLINGER fought to stay on. A climbing wall was easier. It began to swing when she got half way to the fixed ladder. A car drove past and CLINGER hooked her elbows over the rungs and froze, willing the ladder to hold still. Though there was less chance she'd be seen at night, they would certainly report her. Even workmen don't climb water towers after dark.

CLINGER grasped the solid metal rungs above the rope ladder and began to climb. The round ribs of the cage afforded little protection. CLINGER could visualize herself falling, smashing against the sharp bands of metal. It would work like a cheese grater, she decided. If she fell, it would effectively slice off pieces as she rattled around inside on her way to the ground. CLINGER shuddered and tried to focus on the ladder rungs. Climbing walls had ropes above and a harness around her. This was different. She could feel the vertigo of height groping at her legs like a demon pulling her off balance.

A film of sweat covered her palms making her hold tighter than she needed, but fear gave no choice. Half way up, she stopped to rest aching shoulders. Threading her arms through the rungs, CLINGER tried to catch her breath. The ladder tunneled overhead into the cloud of fog. Moisture clung to the ladder rungs up here, and her shoes squeaked on metal. Panic threatened, but she willed herself to keep climbing.

Another car drove past. She could see its lights straining through the fog. CLINGER wanted to call out to them, scream for help.

Instead she kept climbing, trying to pretend it was only a game.

Her hands and feet made a muted, rhythmic clumping on the ladder. At last she emerged onto the narrow catwalk. The waist-high railing felt better suited as a trip wire than a fence, but the second stage ladder was on the opposite side of the water tank.

CLINGER pushed her back against the cold tank and shimmied sideways along the walk. Her legs felt wobbly and uncertain. Steel creaked and her mind started to wander. "Stop it," CLINGER said aloud. She couldn't let herself think. If she did, she'd have a melt down, get stuck up here and then she'd have some explaining to do, for sure.

Neighborhood lights twinkled through the fog. If it weren't for the squeaking, slippery metal and the fear, it might have been a sweet view. CLINGER steadied herself, hand on rail. A stink bug squirmed under her fingers. She recoiled involuntarily and tripped on a brace. CLINGER fell, bouncing off the immovable tank behind her, sprawling to the rusting walkway and slipping underneath the railing. Flailing arms smashed against unforgiving steel, then lashed out, groping for a handhold. Anything to stop the falling. Her hands closed around the ground wire for a lightning rod. Harsh burrs bit into skin. Her face mashed against metal but she held on. Legs dangled, feeling a great emptiness beneath them. They churned, helplessly treading air.

"God help me," she whispered. Her feet—treading air—finally found a ledge. She pushed against it, dragging herself back onto the cat walk. She lay face down, staring at the earth too far away. "I hate this," she said. "I hate this."

After a few minutes CLINGER drew her knees up underneath and crawled toward the second ladder. Fighting against the shake of adrenaline, she forced herself up the last thirty feet, slid onto the top of the tower and lay flat.

CLINGER remembered why she was doing this. She had to finish—had to place the black box.

Wiggling the pack off her back, she fumbled the zipper open and pulled out the plastic box. Using zip ties she fastened the box to one of the antennae.

Then she wormed her way to the ladder, sliding feet first toward the rungs, desperate to get down.

Chapter 29
April 24

Excelsior Energy published an emergency planning packet in accordance with the Nuclear Regulatory Commission. The prevailing authorities on containment and computer-generated scenarios presented the emergency plan in a sterile matter-of-fact manner that made no allowance for reality. The salt and pepper shakers held the map down where it threatened to hump up in the middle. Preston Farwick bit off the pen cap and highlighted all major routes running away from the nuclear reactor. "The Ten Mile Radius is a joke," Preston Farwick said to no one in particular.

Even the Nuclear Regulatory Commission knew it. A nuclear event would start a domino effect. Estimates varied, but most suggested sixty to seventy percent of the population within a fifty mile radius would evacuate. Those closest to the reactor would find their escape routes already in grid lock.

Federal regulations mandated evacuation drills at all schools within a ten-mile radius. The guide provided host schools outside that window responsible to shelter evacuees. Who were they kidding? Farwick thought. At the first hint of real disaster, every teacher with a family would scramble to get their own children out of daycare and run for the hills. School buses would be left without drivers. Students oblivious to the danger would find themselves unsupervised.

Farwick shoved the pen back into the cap and dropped it on the map.

He could picture the noise, the chaos and the panic-birthed violence moving in waves as those fleeing realized every road was already blocked. At almost 800 vehicles per thousand people, there would be way too much metal on the road. The mass evacuation would precipitate more panic. Panic travels faster than vehicles. With their children in the back seats, civilized America would disappear under the fear of radiation poisoning, or worse. Pennsylvania, a state that hosts the world's largest armed force on the first day of hunting season, would now turn their sport to force.

It would be like waking a primeval savage. Now the world would taste the true meaning of his power. Only eight miles downriver of the reactor, his former employer, Evans, Matthew and Fein, would be caught right in the middle. The police department would feel the weight of a whole new kind of evil. They may even want to keep me on after this, but it's too late. I'm freelancing now.

Preston Farwick smiled. Fear. Panic. Chaos. A perfect cocktail. The Moderator would have his vengeance.

Chapter 30
April 25

"Are you going to do it?" Ashley asked.

"I think so. We don't know who it is yet. If I stop playing now, we won't ever know."

"I'm afraid." Ashely bit her lip. "Why the pick-up truck?" she asked.

"I've been thinking about that. I went through the pictures I sent him earlier. That truck is one of the ones I photographed coming out of the nuclear facility."

"Holy shit," her eyes got big. "You think he's trying to blow up the reactor?"

"Nah," Chase replied. "Nuclear facilities are surrounded by fourteen feet of solid concrete. They're built to withstand a direct missile hit. Nothing I could put in the back of a pick-up is going to be big enough to do any real damage. Certainly nothing I can carry."

"When are you going?"

"The Moderator said it has to happen tonight."

"So what is he up to?" she asked.

"Almost everything he's had me doing relates to the nuclear facility."

"Chase. I think we need to talk to the police. This is scary."

"No way. We're getting close now. If we told the police what we were up to, we'd end up in trouble and The Moderator would find other players to pull off whatever he's planning."

"What *is* he planning?" Ashley asked.

"I'm not sure. It's the water tower that has me confused," he replied. "I don't understand why he'd want you to get him pictures of a water tower."

"Right, and what was in that black box?"

"You left it up there, didn't you?"

"Yes."

"Do you think it's still there?"

"No, Chase. I'm not climbing up there again. It's freaky high."

"Of course, not. We have the AR drone, right?"

A flash of understanding crossed her face. "Yes."

"Well then, why don't we take a little virtual field trip?"

"When?"

"I guess we'll have to do it after I drop off the package. Hopefully, we'll figure out what it is in time."

Chapter 31
April 25

The Moderator left the package at the kiln. R8R had no idea how long it had been there, but The Moderator only told him where to find it that afternoon.

After dark, R8R walked past the house where the red pick-up truck was supposed to sit. It wasn't there.

He made a loop and returned by the same route. The truck pulled in. R8R slowed down. An attractive black woman stepped out and walked to the front door, stepping around a toddler's scooter. The porch light went off and the driveway fell back into the companionable shadows of night.

The package was heavier than he anticipated. Running strictly against orders, R8R drew back a corner of the brown waxed paper and stared inside. Twelve cardboard tubes with electronic igniters were packed together in two rows. The tubes looked a lot like homemade rocket fuel cells, but R8R had no way of knowing. He figured his best bet was to place the package, figure out what was on the water tower and call in the police before anything really bad happened.

It was a long shot, and he knew it.

R8R didn't want to think about what might happen if his package contained an explosive. It wouldn't hurt the reactor, but it might hurt the person driving the truck.

He jaywalked across the street, moved quickly to the truck and tucked the package in beneath the silver tool box. It fit perfectly and slid far enough underneath to be hidden from view. He heard a click and realized magnets in the bottom end of the bundle held the package up against the cab, preventing it from sliding back during travel. He had to admit, it was ingenious.

He wished he knew what was in there.

R8R didn't wait around. The last thing he wanted was to get caught. He had a gnawing feeling this game was bigger than the others. He didn't like that they wouldn't be able to explore the box on the water tower again until after dark. He sensed they were running out of time.

Chapter 32
April 25
Late Night

"R8R, really?" Ashley asked.

"Sure. I thought it was a cool name," Chase said.

"What's your other name?"

"RUSH."

Ashley laughed. "That's funny."

"Why?"

"I dunno. I just think you're funny."

"Is that a good thing?" Chase straightened his glasses.

"You make me laugh." She shrugged.

"Then that's a good thing. I love to hear you laugh," he said.

Ashley stared at her friend. Chase always said what he thought. If he thought she looked pretty, he said so. If he liked the way she smelled, he said so. If he thought she was being a dork, he said so. Only he said it nicely.

Chase was like that. Honest, direct, and kind. He didn't play the usual games. He didn't pretend to like things. He wasn't afraid to be smart or curious. He wasn't afraid to say when he didn't know something. She didn't have many friends like that.

Actually, she didn't have any.

"So where do we take off?" he asked.

"There's a concrete slab near the tower. We can set it on that and keep walking. I'll take off as soon as we've moved on."

"Why CLINGER and SAVAGE?" Chase asked. "Did you pick the name CLINGER because you like rock climbing?"

"Not really. I guess I feel like I'm barely hanging on. I'm afraid I'm going crazy like my mom was," Ashley said.

"I thought you said she was better now."

"She is, but I'm afraid I'll turn into what she used to be."

Chase nodded. "I see."

"Why did you pick the name SAVAGE?" Chase asked.

Ashley shrugged; then decided she'd tell him. "Occasionally I feel wild and angry about Lisa. I want to hurt things. Even things I care about." She stopped, trying to find the words. "That's why I'm mean to you somtimes."

She could feel Chase looking at her, but she kept walking. It was the closest she'd ever come to saying she liked him as more than a friend.

Ashley changed the subject. "So what are we looking for up there?"

"I don't know." Chase said, still distracted. "I guess I'll know when I see it."

Chapter 33
April 26
Early Morning

Keys jingled in a pocket. Light poured under the door. Ashley called again. Louder this time but still in another room. The man breathed beyond the door, then spoke his name.

Chase scrambled from bed and wrote the name down. In all caps. He didn't want to forget it this time. Couldn't. He crumpled the paper into a wad. Maybe this time when he woke up, it would be there. Maybe. Ashley screamed.

Chase jolted awake, releasing the sheet from his clenched fist. Finicky got up, turned a circle and settled down again. The green numbers on the digital clock read 3:30 a.m.

He got up and pulled on a sweatshirt. He wasn't going back to sleep. Not after that. Chase flicked on his desk light and turned on the computer. The Moderator was up to something. He needed to know what it was.

Their virtual trip to the top of the water tower yielded nothing. Nothing but a black box strapped to an antennae.   Chase plugged in the jump drive and played it again. Ashely was quite a pilot. The picture was reasonably steady, but the light was poor. Ashley navigated from the view screen on her phone, taking it slow to account for the delay in the drone's wifi signal, orienting the craft with neighborhood lights. Once it reached the top, the picture disappeared between bursts of red light from the tower's warning beacon. The image on the screen flashed on and off at one second intervals.

Chase clicked *pause*. The black box clung to the base of a radio antenna. Maybe it was a transmitter, Chase mused. That would account for why it needed to be mounted on a tower. Maybe it transmitted a parasite signal over the antenna to which it was attached. Chase stared at the screen. What kind of signal? The box had no power input. He'd even asked Ashley about it. So whatever was inside had to be battery-powered.

That meant it was designed for specific time target.

So what did the signal operate? Chase restarted the recording . The image drifted as the quad copter panned the tower. He clicked *pause* again. A hat-like shape rested near the center of the tower's top. Chase zoomed in, but the picture pixilated before slowly resolving itself. He'd seen it before. Somewhere else. He was sure of it.

Think Chase, think. He told himself. The clock blinked to 4:00 a.m.

Then Chase remembered and felt cold inside. The hat was a siren. Part of a network of sirens installed to warn the area in the event of an incident at the Three Mile Island nuclear power plant.

The Moderator wanted control of the warning sirens. The stakes had gone up. Way up.

Chase stuffed himself into a pair of jeans and yanked on a sweatshirt. He put Finicky on a leash and grabbed his coat on his way out the door. It didn't matter what time it was, he had to get back the game camera.

Chapter 34
April 26

The Moderator accessed the control panel from his secure site. It was fairly simple. The control panel served as switchboard for his final play. He checked the indicators. Cell connection for the remote igniters came on-line right on time. The timer activation had been set for 5:30. The cell-phone jammer included on the pick-up truck package wouldn't turn itself on until he told it to.

Everything else looked good.

Now he needed to prime the pump. He pirated his way into a music video channel with over 43 million subscribers. The Moderator selected a clip waiting on his dash board and uploaded it to Youtube. "This should get the ball rolling," he said.

It was going to be an interesting day in the office. Preston Farwick smiled. "Cookie, you wanna come?"

The dog bounded to the front door and sat whimpering with excitement.

"I know how you feel, Cookie. I know just how you feel."

Chapter 35
April 26
5:00 a.m.

Finicky skipped along beside Chase Hikeman, sniffing happily at every telephone pole before the slack disappeared from the leash and Chase dragged him to the next one. Chase could feel his heart pounding. Going back to the apartment to ask for his game camera was nothing compared to his fear about what The Moderator was up to.

A police car drove past. He hoped the 'my-dog-has-to-pee' story would hold if the police wanted to know why he was walking around at this time of the morning. He didn't have a choice. He had to get the camera. Hopefully, the woman hadn't deleted his pictures. Chase chided himself for not having the courage to get it in the first place.

He turned the corner and tried to figure out what he was going to say. "I put a spy camera under your stairs. Can I have it back?" It sounded ridiculous.

But his mind kept drifting back to the transmitter and sirens on the water tower.

Finicky's little legs trotted eagerly beside him. At the bottom of the apartment stairs, Chase tied the leash to the railing. "Sit, Finicky."

The dog complied and cocked his head curiously as Chase ascended the stairs. Here goes nothing, he thought.

The welcome mat read, "Touch it and die."

"Great," Chase muttered. He pushed the doorbell before he could change his mind. Nothing happened. Nothing moved inside. He opened the storm door and knocked. Then he started pounding. This was bigger than his own fear.

A light finally blinked on. Chase kept knocking. "Hurry up," he whispered. "This is an emergency."

A girl opened the door to the end of a security chain. "What do you want?"

"Your boyfriend isn't trying to spy on you," Chase said.

"What the hell are you talking about? Do you know what time it is?"

"Yes. I wouldn't be here if it weren't important. A little while ago I put a camera under your porch. You found it. I heard you arguing with your boyfriend. It was mine, but I was afraid to tell you."

The girl stared at him. He couldn't tell if it were making any sense to her. She looked him over and decided he wasn't scary looking. "You'd better come inside. You're letting the cold air in."

She closed the door to unlatch the chain then held it open. Her nightshirt echoed with a refrain from the welcome mat with 'touch it and die' printed across the front. Chase pushed his glasses up and tried to figure out how to make her understand what he was talking about.

Before he could get started, she turned to a side table and said, "Is this what you're babbling on about?"

Chase had to stop himself from grabbing it out of her hand.

"Yes, that's it." Relief flooded over him.

"You've got a really strange way of introducing yourself to girls," she wrinkled her forehead and sank down in the couch, tucking her legs underneath the night shirt to stay warm.

Chase didn't quite know what to say. He hoped the pictures were still there.

She hugged a pillow and pointed to the couch next to her. "What about my boyfriend?"

Chase had no choice; she still had his camera. He sat down. "Yes," he swallowed. "He wasn't spying on you."

"But you were?" She cocked her head and ran fingers through her hair.

"Not exactly. I was looking for someone else."

"Did you find her?"

"Actually, it's a man."

"I see. Awkward." Her eyes got bigger.

"Not like that. He's been bothering kids in the neighborhood. That's all."

"Okay." She gave him a face that said she didn't believe him. "Well?"

"Well what?" Chase asked.

"Did you find him?"

"It would be on the camera." Chase pointed at it.

"It isn't very big." She turned it over in hand. "Are you sure there're pictures on here?"

"Yes, unless you deleted them."

"Can I see them?"

"You haven't looked at them already?"

"How would I? I don't know anything about spy cameras."

"It's actually a wild-game camera," Chase explained, trying to be patient. "It detects motion using a passive infrared sensor. It sees movement up to 40 feet. May I?"

Chase moved a little closer. "It was set to take pictures for ten hours. Once it detects movement, the camera takes pictures every five seconds." Chase pushed the power button. The three inch screen on the back of the camera blinked to life. She leaned in, more comfortable being close to a high school boy than he was being close to young woman in pajamas.

The pictures flashed by. The camera captured several people in the alley the day Ashley dropped the pictures out the bathroom window. A woman walked past, but it looked like her hands stayed in her pocket. Because of the five-second lapse, Chase couldn't tell if she had picked up anything.

Several others appeared. Mostly runners and baby walkers. Chase knew he couldn't rule them out, but none of them felt right. He remembered what Ashley said about expecting him to look evil or guilty. Chase tried to re-order his expectations. The bad guy probably wasn't going to look guilty.

A man in a long coat appeared on the screen, walking his dog. The man's face stayed hidden, but his German shepherd posed beautifully for the camera as if showing off its Rastafarian collar. A possible, but nothing he could work with.

"That him?" she asked.

"I don't know."

"What do you mean? Don't you know what he looks like?"

"No." Chase didn't explain.

"You are a strange one," she said.

She lost interest in the camera and shook a cigarette from an almost empty pack. "Give me a light?" she asked.

"Um." Chase looked up from the camera. "No, sorry."

"Right over there, dummy." She pointed to an end table.

He handed her the lighter and stood up. "Thanks for the camera."

"Sure," she shrugged.

"I have to go."

Chase slipped the camera into his pocket.

"You know," she said when he got to the door "you really shouldn't go knocking on girls' doors in the early morning. Who knows what they might think?"

"Right. Sorry." Chase fumbled for the door knob and stepped out into the cold morning.

The camera was a waste. Now they didn't have a single lead.

Chapter 36
April 26
6:00 a.m.

Of course, her dad had to answer the door, Chase thought. Not that he really expected Ashley to be out of bed.

"Good morning, Chase. It's awfully early. Everything okay?"

"Not exactly."

"Why don't you come in? Ashley's still sleeping." Pastor Philip Blithe looked knowingly at the microwave clock.

"I know."

The pastor wore a white undershirt over blue twill trousers. And slippers. A flannel housecoat hung loosely from his shoulders. One of the ties dragged along the floor behind him.

"You drink coffee?" Chase didn't really want coffee but nodded anyway.

The pastor poured a mug full. "Cream and sugar are on the table. Why don't you sit down and tell me what's on your mind?"

Chase didn't know where to start. How could he tell Ashley's dad that he'd involved his daughter in the game responsible for Lisa's death? Best to start at the beginning.

"It's kind of a long story."

"Don't you have school today?" he asked.

Chase had forgotten all about it. "Yes, but I'm not going."

The matter of fact reply stumped the pastor. "I see."

"Ashley and I have been playing the game."

His eyebrows knit together. "What game?"

"The Moderator's game."

The pastor stiffened. Ashley had told him a little about it. Enough that he vaguely understood its connection to the bullying that precipitated Lisa's death. "Go on."

Chase spared no details. He explained everything; the player's loop they'd created by pretending to be multiple people for The Moderator's game; the tasks they'd carried out for The Moderator in hopes of finding out who he was.

Chase ended with his recent visit to the girl's apartment to retrieve the game camera. When he finished, he realized he hadn't touched his coffee.

Pastor Blithe chewed his lip like Ashley did when she was thinking.

"Chase, I have a piece of advice for you."

"What's that?" Chase felt relieved.

Pastor Blithe stood up and walked around the table until he was standing over him.

Chase felt a ringing in his ears. He felt his shoulders tense. A rebirth of old fears spawned in the haze of early childhood. The pastor leaned in close. He could smell coffee on Pastor's breath. "Chase, I've made a terrible mistake."

"How so?" Chase asked.

"I made the mistake of asking you to be Ashley's friend." The pastor's words were soft, but he was seething. "A real friend would never have asked her to do those things. Starting today, this friendship is over."

"I thought you had some advice," Chase whispered. His mind stumbled over what the pastor's words.

"I do. Leave my house. Go to the police. Leave Ashley out of this." Pastor Blithe walked to the front door and opened it. "And never speak to my daughter again."

Chase stood; his legs felt wobbly. This couldn't be happening.

He stared uncomprehendingly at the pastor. The man's face left no doubt; he meant every word.

Chapter 37
April 26
6:25 a.m.

The music video started.

Dancers stood frozen on the darkened, smoky stage, black leather stretched tight over lithe bodies. Smoke and blue lights froze in momentary anticipation. A drum beat out a deep tempo.   The sound reverberated, bass drum echoing around the studio. A long note joined the sound, building until the music exploded on stage. Only then did the dancers move. Cameras zoomed in.

A special effects engineer pumped another band of fake smoke across the platform. The dancers moved in air.

Then the music stopped and the image collapsed into static. A voice-over interrupted. A voice that had obviously been altered. It repeated three words over and over.

Terror repeats itself.

A yellow and black symbol slowly resolved from the static background—the black and yellow winged radioactive warning. It grew in clarity and intensity. All the while, the same three words repeated over and over again.

Terror repeats itself.

Terror repeats itself.

The screen cut to black where three new words faded in. Throbbing red and threatening:

REMEMBER

THIS

DAY?

Behind the words arose the long low wail of an air raid siren. Solemn. Surreal. And insistent.

Within minutes, the channel creators were notified their site had been hacked. A complaint was filed with the channel's web host. A polite, automated email informed them they would receive a reply in less than twenty-four hours.

The channel's fans sent the clip viral. Along the way, someone did a web search: *April 26 Radioactive.*

The top hit referenced the April 26 disaster at Chernobyl. The fan posted his findings and the comment section exploded. Top news agencies on the lookout for viral clips tapped in. Five minutes later the clip cued up with a talking head who'd made a call to the nuclear regulatory commission where a secretary assured them she would have the director look into it when he reported to work.

Along the way, a computer geek called in claiming to have traced the post to south central Pennsylvania. Local news stations across the Susquehanna Valley picked up the story. April 26, 1986. The anniversary of the explosion at Chernobyl. The talking heads remembered their own nuclear incident in Pennsylvania a few years earlier: Three Mile Island. April 1. 1979.

The clips made their way onto radio. Ultra-conservative groups and paramilitary militia organizations vied to give their opinion and rendering of the clip, which was now being labeled a 'nuclear threat.'

Chapter 38
April 26
6:45 a.m.

Lisa's blind, white eyes stared out from the coffin. Bloody saliva bubbled up between clenched teeth. Gripped by the seizure, Lisa's fingers twisted into claws. Ashley screamed when the lid closed. Her screams followed the coffin into the earthen hole and woke her up.

She tumbled out of bed, desperate to run away from the horror. But the nightmare followed Ashley into her day. Once again, she wished she could change the channel. Wished she could turn off the pictures in her mind.

Ashley stumbled to the bathroom and started the shower. The shuttle van would arrive soon for the forty-five minute commute to school. Commuters didn't have to report for first period study hall. Hot water helped. Fear that she might be losing her mind kept her moving through the drill of getting ready. She toweled off and pulled on her uniform. Her hair would have to dry on the way.

The thought of going to school and seeing people seemed intolerable. But staying home with her mind doing what it wanted was worse.

The bathroom window steamed over, but it looked bright outside. Ashley drew a cross in the condensation and whispered a prayer for help. She wasn't sure she believed in God anymore, but today she could use any help she could get.

She looked down at her legs, realized they needed a shave. Screw it, she thought. She didn't care. Ashley could feel the horror pull back as her mind started to get busy. Good, she thought.

How was she supposed to keep Lisa's memory alive without it driving her mad?

Maybe Chase would know.

Chase. She wondered what he was doing. After they'd surveyed the tower, he was unsettled. Even afraid. It wasn't like him.

Chapter 39
April 26
6:48 a.m.

"Did you see the news, Chief?" Farwick poked his head into Gregson's office.

"Not yet," he replied. "Why? Anything exciting?"

Farwick let out a snort. "Depends on what gets you going. They're saying a quack released an online video making veiled threats about a nuclear incident."

"What? A terrorist?"

"Something like that. They're saying this guy is local."

"Local?"

"Yep. Apparently it's the anniversary of Chernobyl's accident. Might be worth keeping an eye on."

The phone rang. Gregson held up a finger to Farwick. "Hold on a minute." He picked up the receiver. "Yes?"

The Chief glanced out the window then stared hard at Farwick. He hung up. "You're a step ahead of me, Farwick. That was the state police. They've put us on alert. Keep an eye on this. See what you can uncover."

"Will do."

Chapter 40

April 26

6:53 a.m.

"Shouldn't you be getting ready for school?" The receptionist eyed him suspiciously through thick security glass. The voice hole reminded Chase of Darth Vader's mouth.

"I'm homeschooled," Chase lied.

"Okay." She didn't look convinced. "And who did you need to see?"

"Officer Dixon." Chase figured Dixon might be willing to listen. The officer had been nice enough to them the last time they broke the law trying to track down The Moderator. He wished he had time to get Ralph. After all, Officer Dixon was Ralph's neighbor.

"He's not in; you'll have to come back later."

Chased pushed his glasses up and tried not to let his voice shake. "It's urgent."

"Let me check his schedule."

The glass doors into the station stayed locked unless the secretary pushed the release. Chase needed to get inside. He leaned on the counter and waited. He could hear indistinct chatter from the officers and staff beyond the glass security doors.

A man walked by on the other side of the security doors carrying a cup of coffee. He looked back over his shoulder and called, "Cookie, come." Chase heard the words clearly, though they sounded far away, muffled by glass. A police dog rounded the corner and came trotting after him. They disappeared together into an office down the hall.

The secretary looked up from her monitor. "Come on through. Officer Dixon should be here in a few minutes."

Chase heard the buzzer opening the security doors for him to enter. He froze for an instant before retreating out the main doorway, escaping into the cold spring sunshine.

The German shepherd wore a collar with three stripes. The three colors representative of the Ethiopian flag: green, gold and red.

The colors of the Rastafari.

Chapter 41
April 26
6:55 a.m.

Chase Hikeman sprinted out of the police station and around to the back. He had to catch Dixon before the officer went inside.

Dixon pulled in to the employee parking. Chase waited for him to step out of the car.

"Officer Dixon," Chase said. He wasn't sure the man would remember him. "I'm Chase, Ralph's friend. I was one of the guys who was trying to find The Moderator."

Dixon shut the car door and glanced toward the back door of the station. He was in a hurry. "Sure. What's up?"

Chase swallowed. How could he explain? "I think I've found him."

"Listen, things are hopping this morning. I've got to keep moving. Why don't you come inside, and file a report."

"I can't," Chase said.

"Why not?"

"Because you work with him."

Dixon blinked hard. "Excuse me?"

Chase looked around, expecting the man to appear at any minute. "Who's the police officer with a dog?"

"We don't use dogs here," Dixon replied.

"But I saw a dog in there," Chase pointed toward the station.

"You've been inside already?"

"Yes. I saw the dog."

"What dog?"

"The Moderator's dog." This wasn't going well, Chase thought.

"Chase, we don't use dogs here."

"Then why was a dog in there?"

Understanding spread across Dixon's face. "Oh, you must have seen Preston Farwick's dog. He's not a police officer."

"He's The Moderator." Chase didn't know how else to say it.

Dixon made a face. "Listen, Chase. Preston is a friend of mine. I've known him for a long time. He's clean. You're barking up the wrong tree, no pun intended." Dixon put a hand on his shoulder. Chase flinched. "You've been playing too many games." Dixon said.

"But it's him," Chase persisted.

Dixon stopped with his hand on the back door. "It's a really bad idea to start pointing fingers when you don't know what you're talking about."

The officer keyed himself into the station. The metal door clanged shut behind him. The sign read, 'Employees Only.'

Chapter 42
April 26
6:57 a.m.

Cilene Grove pulled up to the security gate and waited. On time, but barely. One of these days the company would offer on-site daycare.

Patti stepped from the guard hut and ran over to her window, shivering with excitement. "The Feds have called. We're on a threat level."

"Really? What for?"

"A terrorist threat."

"Again?"

"Well, they think this might be for real."

"Great. That should spice up the day."

"Sure beats a normal Monday!" Patti chirped.

Another car pulled up behind. "Gotta go. I don't want to make you late."

Patti ran back to the guard shack and opened the gate. Cilene pulled through and fished in her handbag for lip gloss. Using her rear view mirror, she drew on the gloss. Cilene parked in spot twenty-three. The breeze blew unobstructed from the river across the parking lot. A nuclear facility needed lots of water, after all. But the wind here was always colder. She hurried toward the main entrance to clock in. She pointed her key fob behind her as she left and pushed the button.

The red pick-up truck chirped and the lights flashed once.

Chapter 43
April 26
7:25 a.m.

From his desk, The Moderator dialed a code into his phone, activating the cell phone jammer and remote igniters on the smoke bombs. The range on the cell jammer wasn't great, but it would be enough to keep facility employees from telling the world what was really happening.

Inside the brown-paper wrapping, fuses came to life, hissing like sparklers toward the white substance. As soon as the flame hit the wax-hardened potassium sulfate and sugar, a feral smoke poured out. Within seconds the red pick-up truck disappeared under the swarming cloud. The plume thickened and lifted on the breeze. Other fuses caught, feeding the ballooning mass.

A passing driver noticed the heaving cloud. He'd been listening to news reports about the nuclear threat. The sight of smoke at the reactor gave him a chill.

He grabbed his phone. Must be a dead spot, he reasoned and kept driving until the bars returned. Then he pulled over and called 911.

The incident showed up on firefighters' phones with apps to track every fire in the county. Local firemen hit the blue lights and sped to their stations.

The driver hung up, took a picture and posted it. Then he tweeted: *Smoke at #TMI #Remember the date*. He included a link to the picture.

In three minutes, it was re-tweeted over 600 times. When the firemen donned their gear, the tweet began bouncing around in the millions.

People started to pay attention.

At 8:19 a.m. The Moderator sent another series of numbers through the onion router. Principals and administrative offices within a ten-mile radius of the station received automated calls directing them to initiate nuclear evacuation procedures. This was not a drill.

The news electrified Florin Police station. Station phone lines went hot. Officers scrambled. Chief Gregson dismissed all nonessential staff. Off-duty police officers were called on duty. They dispatched en masse. Every single cruiser hit the road.

At 8:25 a.m. The Moderator dialed in a final sequence. The code reached the transmitter sitting in a black plastic box atop a water tower on the outskirts of Florin. The black box came to life, silently broadcasting the nuclear incident siren activation signal. The newly installed ACS T-128's awoke. The long scream of ninety-two sirens pierced the countryside.

This was not a drill.

On a hill three miles away, a middle school principal set down her phone and took a breath. She lifted the receiver again, pushed the button and sent out the all-call to a school full of kids who were just settling in for the day.

Teachers grabbed attendance rosters, hustled kids into lines, and turned off lights. With practiced unison, teachers and students evacuated. Kids streamed from classrooms, marching toward exits in lines. Teachers grabbed snippets of news from each other on the way. This wasn't scheduled, was it? They turned on their phones and started getting news, tweets and text messages in earnest.

Some had heard the talking heads that morning. *April 26. Remember the date.*

A few teachers slipped out of line and bolted for their cars to get their own kids out of daycare. Students hustled onto buses parked in long strings.

More calls. More texts.

This was not a drill.

More teachers deserted. Family first. Tires squealed as cars careened out of the parking lot, desperate to get ahead of school buses. Three drivers abandoned buses in favor of their own cars. The yellow beasts lay immobile, blocking the way for others.

The exodus had begun.

Chapter 44
April 26
8:27 a.m.

Word travels fast. Though some stations reported an all-clear from the nuclear facility, the real story lay in the mushrooming panic. Panic begets panic. Given the daily diet of scandal, disappointment and ridiculousness reported from Washington, the general population didn't trust the government to tell the truth.

Better to be wrong and safe, than wrong and dead.

Outside the ten-mile zone, people began to move. Bosses looked the other way as employees fled. Abandoned printing presses spat white paper into empty rooms under buzzing fluorescent lights.

Fast-food restaurant managers threw the switch on deep fryers. A few remembered to lock doors on their way out.

Parents reporting to daycare centers found rooms full of children without supervision. The staff had already gone. Parents cursed loudly and hustled their children into SUV's pulled haphazardly onto curbs out front. Children's window-art hung like tokens of another time.

And underneath it all, persistent air-raid sirens blared their declaration: This was not a drill.

By 8:27, feeder routes to main evacuation arteries for the ten-mile zone had jammed. Drivers pushed their way down exit ramps, forcing oncoming traffic onto the berm. It was time to get the hell out of Dodge.

Here and there, violence erupted on roadways. One man held a van at gunpoint, forcing an entire family to disembark. His own vehicle sat belching smoke from an overheating radiator. A pug-nosed dog, dragged reluctantly on its tether, followed him into the van before they raced off.

The wail of police sirens added to the general pandemonium.

Speculations posted and tweeted and texted were confirmed by repetition.

A cancer patient blocked a key intersection and demanded exorbitant tolls. He figured he didn't have long anyway. One young man protested and was shot dead. The rest paid up quickly. By 8:35 a.m. he'd taken in over $800 in cash and stolen credit cards with a combined limit totaling over $200,000.

Off-ramps jammed as people pushed back exiting traffic, forcing themselves the wrong way down highways. A green sport utility vehicle t-boned a grey sedan, backed up and kept going. The driver watched the SUV pull away. A sticker on the back of SUV proclaimed, 'World's Best Soccer Mom.'

CH-47 Chinook twin rotor helicopters thumped overhead. Army reserves were put on notice at the first hint of terrorist activity in and around the nuclear facility. Troops deployed to major intersections wore biohazard masks and hoods. The ghoulish masks heightened awareness, increased levels of concern and served as a catalyst for the burgeoning panic.   This was not a drill.

Chapter 45
April 26
8:31 a.m.

Five floors underground, the pathogens of Evans, Matthew and Fein's Biohazard Level 4 lab crouched in glass caves, hungry, waiting and desperate to find a host. The pathogens in Fifth Lab were special. All were deadly. All untreatable. In effect, the Fifth Lab was a zoo. Even if the scientific community couldn't decide whether or not viruses fell into the category of living or dead, they were treated with more care than the most dangerous wild animals.

The Fifth Lab had active contracts to supply viruses for study to over three hundred private and government labs worldwide. Fifth Lab specialized in hemorrhagic fevers. They colonized Bolivarian, Argentine, and the Crimean-Congo viruses for shipment. The collection included Marburg, Ebola and Lassa.

Working under the secrecy of a government contract, the actual nature of the work in the Fifth Lab remained unknown to the community at large. But every day, new batches of deadly virus were prepared for shipment. Clear glass vials nesting carefully in Styrofoam storage racks were slipped into biosafety plastic bags and sealed in aluminum thermoses. After decontaminating the container exteriors, these were slotted into special coolers designed to keep the virus alive until it reached its destination.

Government guidelines defined in-house security measures which were maintained to withstand assaults from intruders. Tedious transportation policies mandated strict recording and documentation procedures in compliance with the *Infectious Substances Shipping Guidelines,* as published by the International Air Transportation Association, and the use of licensed couriers.

The workers in Fifth Lab received word of the nuclear evacuation via the in-lab intercom system.

Page 143, section 7.5 of the lab's Policies and Procedures manual detailed the specifics for complete shutdown. Complete shutdown involved a systematic and meticulous procedure to kill and destroy all biological agents. Because the pathogens lived in individual glass worlds, every sample had to be moved from storage to the kill oven where it was burned, the only sure way of destroying a sample.

Bio-hazard labs don't shut down easily or quickly.

The Policies and Procedures manual did not, however, cover nuclear contingencies. The scientists who worked in positive pressure suits were used to working under stress and threat. But, as with any job, the task of managing and propagating viruses that looked like nothing more than smears in a petri dish became normal. Scientists daily left the double air-lock, completed the ritual decontamination shower and ultra violet light treatment to manage any potential release. Even the shower water was superheated and sterilized before being released into the municipal septic system.

The viruses could be exterminated, should the need arise. But nuclear radiation was different.

And the scientists knew it. As soon as they received the news, lab work ceased, dangerous live samples were returned to freezers. The Laboratory Director initiated only basic security measures. After all, no one was trying to get in here. He shouted over the hiss of pressure suits. "Get the hell out of here, people. Go. Go. Go."

The daily shipment, already prepped, sat forgotten in its locker upstairs, ready for the courier.

A courier that—today—would never arrive.

Chapter 46
April 26
8:14 a.m.

Ashley's van never made it to school. The driver received a text just before they arrived and wheeled around, speeding back the way they came.

"What's going on?" Ashley asked.

Gravy gripped the wheel with both hands and glanced back at her. "There's an incident at Three Mile Island." Ashley had never seen a grown man really afraid before. It unnerved her.

"Wait. Then shouldn't we be going the other direction?"

"I have to get my kids. Sorry," he shrugged. He looked at Ashley then to the back seat where the other two girls were slumped down with ear buds blocking out the real world. They were oblivious. "If you want, I can let you out here. It's farther away from the reactor. Your call."

Ashley bit her lip. "Oh, my God. Chase," she whispered. "I'll go back," she said.

The driver forced his way through thickening traffic. The shuttle company was only a few blocks from Ashley's home. Traffic careened toward them, driving the wrong way down the highway. Gravy's shoulder tensed and his knuckles went white on the wheel, but he kept going. When the volume of wrong way traffic blocked the road, he swerved onto the grassy berm as if that was why it was there. The van rattled and bounced and the girls in the back seats woke up.

"What's Gravy doing?" one yelled.

Ashley faced her and replied, "He forgot something."

The girl gave her a you've-lost-your-freaking-mind look.

"Gravy!" the girl shouted, "What the hell?"

Gravy shot Ashley a look in the rear view mirror. "You explain. My offer stands."

Ashley relayed the story to the girls in the back. They both wanted out.

Gravy slammed on the brakes. They slid to a stop, leaving muddy skid marks behind the van. The girls tumbled out and Gravy had the tires spinning before they hit the ground. The tartan-clad teenagers stared after them—two baffled cheerleaders marooned on a highway.

Ashley pointed ahead to a blocked exit ramp. "You can't get through up there." A tractor-trailer attempted to drive over the hump between lanes in an effort to break out of the snarl. The turn was too sharp and the truck's trailer rode up over the hood of a Mini. It must have happened recently. A middle-aged woman was on foot, running down the center of the highway. Ashley guessed she'd been the driver of the car. No one was taking the time to swap insurance information today.

Gravy pulled the van to a stop to study his options. He slipped the van into reverse and drove back the way he had come without turning around. The two girls saw the white van returning and ran toward them.

"Gravy, watch out!" Ashley yelled. He was going to run them down.

"I see them," he replied. "Hang on."

Gravy braked and jammed the car into another slide on the wet grass. Gears ground as he forced the transmission back into drive. Cranking the wheel hard to the right, Gravy pushed the van across the berm and toward a logging track that ran over the hill beside the road.

Too late for a seat belt, Ashley grabbed the 'oh-crap' bar overhead and tried to keep herself from bouncing into the roof. The van plunged through the uncut grass at the far edge of the highway cut. The van's shocks bottomed out hard, as the tires shot over a mound of hardened earth left from the original grading. They surged forward, climbing through the scrub trees of a young forest.

Another vehicle tried to follow them up the trail. Its front end hit the mound and stopped, sending up a cloud of steam. Ashley's classmates stood bewildered and angry beside it at the bottom of the hill.

Gravy didn't slow down.

"Will we make it?" Ashley's eyes were big. The track was barely visible. Leaves and loose shale made the back end of the van swing as it rounded corners.

"I don't know. It has the same chassis as a full size pick-up, but I wouldn't try to drive one of those up here unless I had a good reason."

Ashley stared ahead, transfixed by their desperate race up the hill. Fine spring leaves blushed the smaller trees in the woods, but the big ones stood naked. "Look out!" Ashley screamed.

Gravy swerved too late. A low slung branch slapped the windshield. Glass spidered, and the van lurched to a stop. The shield sagged uselessly in place like a fish net —impossible to see through.

"You okay?" Gravy asked without looking back.

Ashley's eyes were wide. "Fine." This guy was crazy.

Gravy unbuckled his belt, wiggled from his seat and kicked the broken window out of its moorings. The popcorn pieces of glass scattered across the dash. Back in his seat, Gravy launched the van forward again, climbing ever higher, following the logging track up to the brow of the hill. Damp cold air swept in where the window had been. Not for the first time, Ashley cursed her tartan skirt. Her legs were freezing. At the summit, the floor of the woods opened to bracken. The track disappeared into a meadow of fern.

Gravy leaned over the steering wheel trying to make out the trail.

"So much for our road," he yelled.

Ashley nodded and hung on. Tears streamed down her face from the cold wind in her eyes, but she blinked them away as if Gravy needed her eyes open so he could drive.

Gravy pushed forward, aiming for places where the van might fit through trees. The side view mirror hung by wires on the passenger side, looking like a popped out eyeball. When did that happen? Ashley wondered.

The van slewed hard to avoid a fallen tree and a large rock hammered underneath, scraping the length of the van as they passed over it.

Almost immediately, the van got louder.

"I think that was the muffler," Gravy shouted over the racket.

They burst out of the fern meadow. Gravy managed to find the track and the van hurtled through the woods, heading down the other side of the hill.

"There's a creek at the bottom," Gravy yelled.

"What are you going to do?" Ashley asked, but he didn't hear her.

Sure enough, the trees opened up and the track they'd been following straightened out, heading right into the black water of the creek. The creek itself was only fifteen feet wide, but she couldn't see the bottom.

Gravy floored the accelerator and the van roared right for it.

"Holy shit!" Ashley screamed.

The van pounded into the rocky creek. A wall of white exploded up from the impact, cascading in through the window, enveloping Ashley in frigid water as it swept back through the van like a miniature tidal wave. For a few long seconds the drapery of water enveloped them. The howl of the van's exhaust disappeared as quickly as it started. Water slapped up over the front and kissed the doors beneath the window ledge.

Ashley's clothes stuck to her skin, but she didn't care. She wedged her feet under the passenger seat in front of her and willed the van to keep moving. Tires skipped and caught their way across the uneven creek. She could feel them spinning.

"Come on," Gravy muttered. "Keep moving."

Then the van broke from the loose gravel beneath, pushed by the spring waters. Tires spun briefly before they got traction, jerking them hard. The popped-out-eye-ball of the side mirror swung on its wires, splashing in the water.

Gravy let out a snarl and stomped the accelerator.

Impossibly, the van moved against water, pushing back. Tires grabbed, spun and grabbed again. They lurched forward, crawling toward the bank. She couldn't believe it. It was actually moving!

The exhaust bubbled behind, grew into a growling snarl and at last, returned to the full blown howl as the van emerged from the water. They were free.

"Yes!" Ashley yelled.

Gravy winked at her in the rear view. "If you look now, you might see the angels that pushed us out."

Ashley shivered with relief. She barely knew this man, but she sure as hell wished her dad was this determined to save his kids.

Chapter 47
April 26
8:43 a.m.

Preston Farwick listened to the police scanner in his office. He could feel the thrill of power. The mass panic of movement completely disqualified urgent appeals from the nuclear reactor that everything was in order. The constant wail of sirens rotating atop their telephone poles accentuated the general disquiet and awakened primal fear. The energy company that owned the reactor maintained five rumor hotlines in accordance with Federal regulations. The lines contained recorded, repeated messages.

"Let's go, Cookie. Time for my final play."

Farwick's silver van sat alone in the parking lot. Traffic filled Main Street beside the station. With over 400,000 people in the county, the evacuation was just getting started. Horns filled the usually quiet town. There were already too many cars on the road, but traffic was still moving.

"Time to join the fun." Farwick opened the car door and Cookie scrambled excitedly over the driver's seat ahead of him. Farwick entered the traffic. He would cut across town, make his stop, and join the mass migration.

With luck, he would never return.

Cookie sat on the passenger seat, tongue lolling from her mouth as she stared out the window. Farwick chuckled to himself. "This is nothing," he told his dog. "Just wait until they figure out what went missing from Evans, Matthew and Fein."

He turned off Main Street. Traffic here moved a little faster. He passed the library and headed toward the river. On the western horizon the smoke plume billowed from the nuclear plant. It rose white and menacing next to the normal steam from the cooling towers. It worked better than expected and overruled assurances by the reactor's spokesperson that all was well.

"Where there's smoke..." Farwick muttered.

Traffic continued to pour into the melee, fighting to find the fastest way out. A few motorcycles screamed between cars. A four wheeler with three passengers sitting on the front and rear racks, growled its way across open fields. One man decided he would follow them. Soon other vehicles bounced over soggy fields, tires spinning, spraying mud up their sides.

The pop of gunshots punctuated horns and sirens. Any road heading away from the reactor snarled as perfectly as a street in downtown Bombay.

Farwick picked his way toward the lab.

Chapter 48
April 26
9:12 a.m.

The facility parking lot stood empty. All Evans, Matthew and Fein employees had made good their escape. Though they were primarily biologists, scientists understood radiation plumes.

Security must have felt the same way. The empty guard shack sat like a sleeping sentinel along the chain link fence. No sense standing around waiting when everyone in the world, it seemed, was getting away. In-building security staff left with the scientists.

Farwick drove on the grass to avoid the entry boom blocking the way to the parking lot. He parked in a spot reserved for "Sarge." The managing director for the facility reported directly to corporate headquarters in Georgia. The network security Farwick installed months before precluded any way in from the outside. But Farwick hacked into the parking-lot security monitors. From that vantage point, he'd been able to make a complete traffic study.

Within one month of his termination, a new courier service started appearing regularly on the scene. A simple phone call revealed that the courier held certificates from the Department of Transportation to handle Level 3 and 4 Biohazards.

Handling biohazards, even the nasty stuff, was a cake walk next to the red tape required for transporting nuclear fuels. He didn't know exactly what they were shipping out of Fifth Lab, but Preston knew he could turn it into a game changer.

Preston Farwick felt high. The rest of the world had their attention on the nuclear facility a few miles up the road.

He pulled the keys and allowed himself a moment to gloat. Early on, during his tenure at Evans, Matthew and Fein, Farwick duplicated his security pass. At first it was simply to forestall the embarrassment of losing the original key-card. Now that single decision would turn into a windfall. Since then, he'd reprogrammed the card so the system wouldn't identify him.

"Stay, Cookie." Farwick got out. "This shouldn't take long."

Chapter 49
April 26
9:13 a.m.

He wasn't exactly sure why he stowed away. His only thought was that he couldn't let The Moderator get away again. He hadn't even seen the man's face. A silver mini-van sure didn't seem like the kind of vehicle a bad guy would drive. But when it was the last vehicle in the parking lot, and he hadn't seen the dog leave, Chase knew it had to be the one.

As the man drove away from the station, Chase heard him talking and got the same odd feeling he felt when the lap bar came down on a roller coaster he'd rather not be on. Now Chase had no way of getting off the ride.

The van parked and the car door closed. Chase stayed crouched in the trunk, hoping the man didn't need anything back there.

Cookie barked after her master and clawed at the door.

Now or never, Chase thought. He poked his head over the back seat. The man disappeared into the building. Now what?

The dog noticed him and went berserk. Her hackles stood on end, and she barked madly. Chase didn't move. He whistled softly and called to her. "Come here, Cookie." The dog scratched her way to the rear of the van, growling and snarling and sniffing him over until her tail started to wag. Chase liked dogs. Even big ones.

Most dogs liked him, too. He figured it was because he was small and not very threatening. Some consolation. Being big and scary would come in handy right now.

The Moderator's phone sat in the cup holder on the dash. He shoved the dog out of his way and clambered over the seat to reach it. Crouching low, he sent a text to Ashley's number. He didn't know exactly where she was, but he needed help.

Chapter 50
April 26
9:15 a.m.

Gravy dropped Ashley on the sidewalk by her house before speeding off. The dangling side mirror bumped against the door as he pulled away.

The neighborhood felt like a ghost town. The few cars around drove like demons. Everything else was eerily quiet. One bewildered elderly woman walked unsteadily down the road.

Her mom's car sat parked at the curb. Ashley burst through the front door. "Mom! Dad!" She raced through the house, checking the rooms. They weren't there. They must have assumed she was safely out of range of the nuclear facility at school and left in her dad's car.

Even from inside, she could hear the wail of sirens. Ashley swore. She didn't know what to do. She didn't know the first thing about nuclear power plants. She didn't know anything. She needed to find Chase.

"God help me!" The phone buzzed. Her thumb opened the screen. A text from Chase, but she didn't recognize the number.

When did Chase get a phone? She wondered.

"Oh, no!" Ashley moaned and started moving. Chase solved the riddle of the black box. She had to get back to the tower.

Bolting up the stairs to her bedroom, she pulled off wet clothes, dropping them in a pile on the carpet. She slipped on a pair of sweats and climbing shoes without socks. The clothes felt soft and warm after the freezing sticky-wet of a soaked school uniform. She rummaged in the closet to find a bundle of climbing rope then charged back downstairs.

She hit the sidewalk at a run, but stopped and retraced her steps. Why not? She figured. This was an emergency. She could ask for permission later.

The car keys hung on a hook by the door. She yanked them off and sped back to her mom's car. "God, help me figure this out," she whispered.

She turned the key and the car came to life. How hard could it be?

The gear shift wouldn't release. What the hell was wrong with it? She moved to grab hold with both hands. As her foot pushed on the brake the lever slid easily out of park. The vehicle started to roll and she jammed on the brake again.

Where is Gravy when I need him? she wondered. Ashley gingerly pressed the accelerator and pulled away from the curb, heading back to the water tower.

Chapter 51
April 26
9:16 a.m.

Preston Farwick slid his card through the reader and let himself into the building. Fifth Lab could not be accessed from the facility's primary elevator. He hurried down the hallway, slid his card again and pressed the button. Silver doors opened and Farwick stepped inside.

The alternate elevator shaft had been installed to minimize and scrutinize traffic heading to Bio Level 4. He swiped his card again inside the elevator and a keyboard appeared. Password time.

His specialty.

Every good programmer designs a back door. Of course, it rarely paid to inform management. It didn't make much difference when the entire computer system, all its files, networks and software could only be accessed from inside the Lab. But they also put him in charge of installing the password algorithm. He complied and quietly incorporated an administrative access code. Nice.

The doors closed. Overhead fluorescents blinked off and purple UV lights installed vertically in the elevator walls came on. Security and containment systems for bio hazards started here. Virus danger potential was greater for those exiting the lab. A bell dinged and the elevator descended into the seventy-five foot shaft.

He stepped into the research lab, picked a console, plugged in a portable drive and found the most recent back-up file. The copy would take a while, but the data he gathered would sell well on the international black market.

Plenty of time to find what he had really come for.

Thick glass walls separated Level 4 lab from the rest of the room. A huge, ante chamber-like vestibule surrounded the lab on three sides. The air-lock entry door, fitted with decontamination showers and more UV light to kill escaped viruses, backed the fourth side of the inner lab.

The exterior vestibule consisted of multiple computer work stations and pre-lab prep tables. Farwick walked quickly, looking for the courier bag. It should be out here. The courier would certainly not be allowed to enter the inner chamber. It had to be down here.

Chapter 52
April 26
9:18 a.m.

Ashley lurched her way across town to the water tower. The long blue legs supporting the mammoth tank made her feel cold again. She still hadn't forgotten the last slip. The tower ladder only started ten feet off the ground. She hoped the climbing rope she brought would help her reach it. There was no way she could jump the first ten feet to the bottom rung.

She stared at the tower through the car window. The scream of sirens was louder here. She realized the funny shaped hat on top of the tower was making the noise. The siren turned slowly. It reminded her of a World War II movie. Air-raid sirens, search lights fingering dark skies, the distant drone of German aircraft, the whistle of falling bombs, the smell of fear and cordite and the feel-it-in-your-chest thump-thump-thump of anti-aircraft guns.

Gripping the steering wheel, Ashley pulled onto the grass. She'd forgotten about the fence.

The gate was locked. "Damn it," she said. Piercing waves of sound made it hard to concentrate. "Just get it done," she told herself.

Gravy had given her an idea.

She got back into the car. Her mother was going to freak, but right now this was more important. Who needs a rope? She backed up, turned hard toward the tower and aimed for the gate.

Chapter 53
April 26
9:51 a.m.

The file-copy complete, Preston Farwick pulled the disk. Using the back door, he accessed files for the security cameras, created a loop, and erased himself from digital memory. Not that it would matter. What he'd have with him would clear a wide path to go anywhere he wanted.

He'd not been able to locate the courier pack. He realized security regulations probably forbid the shipper from entering any part of the Fifth Lab. The pack must be on the first floor.

He swiped his card and re-entered the elevator, submitting himself again to the party-like black lights. The stainless steel room floated up from the basement.

The doors opened to the industrial green carpet he remembered from his term of employment with the company. Then he saw it. A locker installed outside the administrative office. Any hazardous pathogens would have to be kept secure until the courier arrived. He walked into the adjacent office and rifled through the secretary's desk. Abby had been a fixture at Evans, Matthew and Fein ever since he could remember.

There it was. "Abby," Farwick chided, "you should really be more careful."

Farwick took the key and removed the bio-hazard cooler. It looked like an oversized lunch box. To the casual observer, it would be nothing more than that. Farwick laughed aloud. He would bring the world to its knees.

Chapter 54
April 26
9:52 a.m.

Ashley pressed her hands hard over her ears. It didn't seem to help. She stood on the catwalk of the water tower just below the final ladder. Already it was too loud. The noise made an ache that pulled at the very roots of her ears.

Ashley's pocket vibrated. She glanced quickly at the text and shoved the phone away so she could cover her ears again. She would have to do it now. Chase found The Moderator. She needed to get to him. Quickly.

But she couldn't climb the last stretch of ladder with hands over her ears. Gritting teeth against pain, Ashley scrambled up. The higher she got, the more it felt like hot needles in her eardrums. But the pain kept her focused on destroying the black box, kept her from thinking about falling.

Ashley fought back the urge to let go and cover her ears. She scrambled over the top of the ladder and rolled onto the cold blue surface of the tank, hands pressed against the side of her head. The siren turned slowly and Ashley elbow-crawled to the plastic box she had fastened into place. Rolling onto her back she kicked at the box, trying to break it loose.

The plastic zip ties held firm. It wasn't going to work. On the far side of the tower, a single lightning rod pointed up from the iron railing. Maybe she could pry the box off with that? She squirmed her way over. No way. It wasn't going to come off. She stood and ran back to the black box, her fear of heights pushed aside by the noise drilling into her head. She started kicking at the box again, choking back sobs of pain. The zip ties held, but the box cracked open around a center seam. Waiting until the siren's cone rotated away from her, she let go of her ears and pulled madly at the plastic housing. Even with the siren's cone facing away, the crushing sound made her feel claustrophobic, desperate to get away from its suffocating scream. At last, the housing gave way. She tore at the mysterious bundle of electronics inside the box, yanked it out and launched it over the side.

She ran to the second stage ladder and forced herself to turn around so she could hold on as she climbed. When she reached the cat walk, the shrieking siren began to slow, sliding into a guttural moan before finally coming to rest.

Ashley scrambled down the primary ladder, now keenly aware of another sound. From inside her head came the high-pitched ringing of her ears. It drowned out the clumping of her hands and feet on metal rungs.

She dropped onto the top of her mom's car. Her climbing shoes left a couple of dents in the roof. She slid off and climbed in. Time to find Chase.

Chapter 55
April 26
9:59 a.m.

The air-raid sirens gradually descended to silence. The absence of the constant wailing created a vacuum. Ashley had done it!

She must have received his text. Chase glanced at his watch. It would take her at least fifteen minutes to get to him. Hurry up, he whispered.

He wasn't sure what this facility was, but not every work place sported a security shack at the gate. Chase looked out the rear window and saw tracks through grass where the van avoided the security boom. The Moderator must have planned to come here all along. The lab was well within the nuclear facilities ten-mile radius. There were no people. Even the side road was empty. Cars jammed major evacuation routes. Chase looked up through glass to stare at helicopters thumping overhead. He counted seven. He'd never seen anything like it. It made him shiver.

He'd helped this guy. He'd taken pictures and delivered that package, whatever it was.

What had he done? Started a war?

All along he'd justified it because of Ashley's sister. But he knew the truth. He wanted to help Ashley. He'd wanted to see her come back to life. And he'd wanted another excuse to be near her. It was his idea to create the player loop, and he'd talked her into it.

Ashley's dad was right. He was a fool. He'd brought her into this thing. And it was so much bigger than he'd imagined. Now he was doing it again. The dog turned to the window and looked at the door where her master disappeared. I have to get out of here, Chase thought. He peeked out the side window. Nothing. His fingers scrambled over the trunk door trying to find a release. Where was it?

Chase felt his heart beating. Panic started to set in. He'd felt it before. The same dread he knew when his mom's boyfriend was at the door of his bedroom.

The dog barked. Chase peeked out the window then collapsed into a fetal position in the trunk. The man was walking toward the van. His phone buzzed on the dash and the dog barked wildly at her master.

Sunlight broke through overhead clouds and a shaft cut through the window, changing the color on the carpet next to him. Chase pressed his ear against the floor of the van, willing it to stay closed. He could hear the man's shoes; feel him standing there.

Chase could hear breathing. Keys jangled. Just like his dream. He couldn't move. The man would open the door, and Chase would see The Moderator's smiling face for the first time.

Not that it mattered. Once The Moderator found him, it would all be over.

The phone buzzed again on the console and Chase heard the lock click inside the back door.

Chapter 56
April 26
9:50 a.m.

"I can't get through to the school." Elizabeth Blithe said. "There must be too much cell traffic."

Philip inched along. Red brake lights extended as far as he could see. Every local news station told conflicting reports, but the bad news stories got more traction and the mass panic and helicopters had everyone convinced. This was the real deal.

"I got the family locator option on our phone plan. Look her up. They're probably moving students away from the reactor."

Elizabeth logged onto their provider's website and typed in Ashley's phone number. Soon a small map appeared with a red pin indicating the location of her phone.

"What is she doing?" Elizabeth held the phone out to Philip. "She's back in Florin."

"What do you mean? The school is thirty miles from here!" Philip took the phone from his wife and zoomed in.

The pin showed her location. Then refreshed. Ashley was moving.

"We've got to turn around," Philip said. "I think she'll need our help."

Chapter 57
April 26
9:58 a.m.

The world spun and the ringing in her head wouldn't stop. Ashley fought to concentrate on the screen, forcing herself to focus on tiny letters as she texted a reply to Chase: *On my way.*

Traffic wasn't moving on Main Street so she turned off to cut across the back road. A terrible dizziness accompanied the pain in her ears. Ashley jammed on the brakes, pushed open the driver's door and vomited on the street. Her stomach cramped with the effort. She tucked the hair behind her ears and wiped her mouth on her sleeve. She pulled the door shut and kept going. Had to get to Chase.

Ashley pushed the pedal down, urging the car forward. She rounded a corner and stood hard on the brakes again. Tires squealed as she swerved around a cow ambling across the road. The whole world has gone mad, she thought. Nausea threatened again, but the thought of Chase in danger pushed her on.

The empty road descended toward the river. The whole town exuded an eerie, abandoned feel as if aliens had taken everyone away. She neared the address Chase gave her. A fence surrounded the property, but the building looked like an office or factory. Maybe both. One silver van sat in the parking lot next to a dumpster in front of the building with the brown metal roof.

This was it. She slowed, studying the fence line, trying to find the entrance. The car in the parking lot started to move. She crept along the road, watching it exit the property on the far side. It turned toward her. Ashley scoured the area inside the fence for Chase. This was the place. She was sure of it. As the van pulled past; she sped up and turned into the facility. A large stop sign read, *STOP. This is a biosecure area. No unauthorized entry.*

She ignored it, bounced over the grassy area beside the security boom and cut across the empty white lines of parking spaces toward the front door. She felt uneasy. Chase said he'd be waiting here. She got out and stood, turning slowly in a circle.

"Chase!" Ashley yelled. The ringing in her ears drowned out the sound of her own voice.

She leaned over and vomited the leftovers onto the asphalt. A black penlight lay next to her feet. Chase's! The light was on.

She looked up and saw the silver van disappearing down the road.

"No!" Ashley screamed. She jumped back into the car and raced after it.

Chapter 58
April 26
10:15 a.m.

After taping him up, The Moderator shoved him through the side door of the dumpster, then shut it. A few noodles of daylight poked through rust holes in the bin. Chase listened to the sound of his own breathing.

The foul smell pressed against his skin. He could feel something sharp biting into his back. Another ribbon of light seeped in under the dumpster lid. Chase heard the van drive out of the parking lot. Relief flooded over him. The last thing he wanted now was for Ashley to show up before the man left. Duct tape pulled hair from his arms as he struggled against it. The Moderator was thorough.

Chase wiggled toward the sliding side door. Bags of trash shifted underneath and he settled deeper into them. He lay still and waited for the plastic bags around him to be quiet.

A car door slammed outside. Ashley! It had to be her.

Chase thrashed around in the dumpster, forcing his taped legs down into the trash so he could stand. Slipping and falling, he pressed his face against a rust hole in the dumpster's side. He caught a glimpse of blond hair and let out a muffled yell. The tape over his mouth effectively clamped out the sound. Chase managed to poke a thumb through a gap in his restraint. Bringing hands to his face, he clawed frantically at the tape. The smell and dark and adrenaline fought against him. He found a frayed edge and pulled. It tore at his skin, but he didn't care. He had to get her attention.

"Ashley!" Chase yelled.

He stopped and listened. Nothing.

He called again, louder this time.

Chase tried to use his head to force the lid open. "Ashley!"

He chewed at the tape around his hands and wrists, picking it apart strand by strand. He peeked out. Why wasn't she helping him? She had to hear him.

He shouted again, but she didn't turn, didn't even acknowledge the sound. Maybe she was pretending not to notice him like so many other kids. But that wasn't like her.

Chase gnawed at the tape, finally tearing through the sticky fabric enough to wiggle a hand free. He winced as it pulled hair from his arm.

Chase wrenched off the last of the tape and pulled wildly at the heavy plastic door. It was locked. He pushed his mouth up to the crack and called again. "I'm in the dumpster."

Then Ashley called his name. He lay back against the black plastic bags and breathed a sigh of relief.

She'd found him.

Chapter 59
April 26
10:15 a.m.

"How did she get over to the neighboring town?" Elizabeth held the phone for her husband to see. They bounced along a farm road, scrambling to catch up with their daughter.

Philip glanced at the location. "She must have gotten a ride."

"What for?" Elizabeth asked.

"I have no idea. Is she still moving?"

"No. I don't think so."

"Good." The dash rattled as Philip sped over the rough track. The lane ran between fields of winter wheat before depositing them onto a paved road. Philip turned and accelerated. He came to a fenced-in facility.

"This is the address, but why would she be here?"

He crashed through the security boom and raced into the parking lot.

They pulled up next to the building and piled out of the car.

"Maybe she's inside." Elizabeth suggested.

She ran up to the front entrance and pulled on the door. "It's locked." Shielding the glass with her hands, she peered into the darkened office. "Everyone's gone."

"Check the location again." Philip said. "We have to find her and get out of here. The nuclear facility is too close."

Philip started to jog the perimeter, looking for another entrance when he heard a voice inside the dumpster.

He lifted the bolt locking the side door and slid it open.

"Chase Hikeman," Philip was incredulous. "What are you doing?"

"It's a long story. We have to hurry. I think Ashley is chasing The Moderator."

The Pastor shot him a dangerous look. "You'd better come with us."

Chase climbed out of the dumpster and pulled the last of the tape off his jeans.

"Philip!" Elizabeth ran up to them, holding her phone. "Ashley's moving again."

"How could she have gone that far already?" Philip asked. "She was just here."

"She's got your car," Chase said.

They both looked at the boy.

"She can't drive," Elizabeth protested. "She doesn't have her license."

Philip glared at him. "You've got some explaining to do. You got her into this and now she's out there alone."

Chase pushed at his glasses. "Can I borrow your phone?"

Chapter 60
April 26
10:18 a.m.

Ashley caught up to the van before it turned on the first side road heading toward the river. It drove without urgency and, unlike the rest of the world, didn't seem to be in a hurry to get out of town.

The ringing in Ashley's head continued and the accompanying nausea persisted.

The van threaded past historic colonial architecture, winding its way closer to the river. Ashley fought to focus beyond the pain in her ears, but the van had Chase and she wasn't going to let him get away. She was glad there weren't other cars on the road.

She followed them onto Front Street. What now?

Her pocket vibrated. She grabbed her phone and stared at the screen. In-coming call. Her parents. She punched the button, but realized too late she couldn't make out what anyone was saying.

She shouted into the phone. "Text me. I can't hear anything." She hung up and waited. If it was important, her parents would have to text.

The van turned at a 'boat landing' sign and drove toward the river. She didn't know what to do. She followed at a distance, trying to stay as far back as she could without losing them. The lane turned through a small park. Scrub and brush littered the woods, keeping her from seeing ahead. If only Chase could tell her what to do.

Her pocket vibrated. Dad again. Strange. She parked in the middle of the road, trying to make sense of it. The text was signed by Chase. He said The Moderator had stolen a cooler from the lab. Whatever was inside it was dangerous. Very dangerous.

Her head spun. She thought Chase was in the car up ahead?

Ashley skimmed the text and read it again.

The cooler was what The Moderator was really after.

Ashley dropped the phone on the seat beside her. "Thank God," she whispered. Chase was with her parents.

Another text followed the first from her dad's phone. *DO NOT FOLLOW THE MODERATOR.*

She thumbed her reply. *Okay.*

That didn't sound like Chase, she thought. Then it dawned on her. *The Moderator hacked her parent's phone! Chase wasn't with them!* The Moderator must know she was following and was trying to scare her off.

Her mind flashed to Lisa. She saw the grip of convulsion tighten like iron bands around her sister's middle, heard the stifled scream bubbling up through the bloody saliva, the blank whites of her eyes staring out from fluttering eyelids.

"I don't think so, asshole. I'm not playing the sucker this time." She jammed the car into drive. This was her chance. "You're not getting away now."

The Ford rounded a bend and turned into a parking lot fronting the river. Long parking spaces for cars with boat trailers looked like a line of hash marks across black asphalt. A motorboat moored to a tree rested near the launch.

Ashley gripped the wheel, accelerating around the corner. He'd seen her coming. She hit the van square in the bumper, sending it lurching forward. Ashley followed, tires squealing as she stood on the gas. The car mashed up against the van, propelling it hard into one of the tulip poplars lining the parking lot. She saw the van's airbag deploy. Everything stopped. Her wrists stung with the pain of impact.

"Chase!" She had to get him out of there and away from The Moderator.

Her door stuck; she tried to shoulder it open. It wouldn't budge. She lowered the window and crawled out.

Scrambling over the hood, she opened the rear hatch of the van. "Chase!" she yelled.

The driver, temporarily stunned by the airbag's impact, sat shaking his head. Chase wasn't in there. Ashley covered her ears. The ringing got worse. What the hell was happening?

"Chase!" Ashley screamed.

The driver turned and looked at her over the seats. He looked completely surprised. Had she made a mistake? Were the texts really from Chase?

He reached for his door and Ashley felt the adrenaline crash. Her legs turn to jello—that same horrible feeling she got when chased by unspeakable evil in her dreams. She looked down and saw a red cooler. A single carrying strap lay over the top. On the side was a label. Black on yellow. She blinked and read. "BIOHAZARD."

What the hell had she done? Maybe Chase *was* with her parents? The puzzle pieces too-slowly rearranged themselves in her mind.

The van door opened. The man was getting out.

In a flash, she remembered the text from Chase. The lab. The cooler.

Without thinking, she grabbed the strap on the bag and started running.

Chapter 61
April 26
10:21 a.m.

Philip Blithe drove like a man possessed. Elizabeth shouted directions and Chase slewed across the back seat as they careened around corners.

"Turn here!" Elizabeth shouted and pointed to a road leading back toward the river. Tires squealed as Philip yanked the wheel to the right. Trees growing close to the road flashed past Chase's window before they emerged into the parking lot.

Their car and a silver van lay like spent dominoes, mashed against each other, doors open and empty. Steam poured from the sedan's radiator and a flaccid airbag hung from the center of the van's steering wheel. Door alarm bells pinged incessantly in both vehicles, parroting each other.

Ashley's parents hovered over their phone, trying to locate Ashley, but her marker wasn't moving. The found the phone laying on the floor of the car. The sedan's fenders wrinkled back in a tired smile and keys hung in the ignition. Ashley was gone.

Chase looked around. He saw the boat The Moderator planned to use for a getaway. Good, he thought. They must be nearby. He shot a glance into the van's trunk. Empty.

An abandoned rail cut followed a derelict canal. Chase took off running.

Ashley's parents called after him, but he ignored them. The dinging of cars fell behind and Chase could hear only the *ffft* of gravel underfoot and his own breathing. The rail path ran parallel to the river and beneath Chickies cliff. This area once housed one of the largest Indian villages. Its cliff dominated the 440 acre park.

Chase rounded a bend and saw them ahead. Ashley had started climbing. The Moderator reached up to grab her foot. The red cooler flopped around on Ashley's shoulder, throwing her off balance.

Chase tried not to think what might happen if it dropped. He raced toward the man and slammed into his lower back. Together they rammed into the iron-hard rock. The man's face struck the wall just as his fingers wrapped around Ashley's foot. She pulled free and climbed out of reach.

Chase knelt on the ground. His fingers scrambled over the gravel, groping for his glasses. He heard The Moderator curse. The man's face was fuzzy and unclear.

"Chase, look out!" Ashley screamed.

The kick landed hard under Chase's chin. Shards of light ricocheted around his brain. His head snapped back, and he fell on unforgiving stone. Pain seethed spread like hot lava around

the sides of his head. The tunnel of light started to close in. "No!"
Chase fought against it. He couldn't pass out. Not now.

Working by feel, Chase rolled toward the man and wrapped
himself around his feet, determined to let Ashley get away.

Something hard smashed into the back of Chase's head and the
light went out. Chase held on as long as he could. For a few more
seconds, Chase could hear Ashley screaming, then her voice faded
and blackness carried him away.

The boy slumped at his feet. Preston Farwick shook him off. Fissures crisscrossed the cliff that towered above. The girl climbed further out of reach.

"You have no idea what you're carrying," he shouted.

She didn't answer, but seemed intent on going the whole way to the top. The exposed anticline extended two hundred feet overhead. He reached up, found a hand hold and started to climb after her. There was no way he would let her get away with his prize. The climb started out simple enough, and he managed to shorten the distance between himself and the girl.

After a few minutes, he drew level with the power lines running along the river behind him. The Susquehanna spread out like a massive black snake. The boy lay unmoving on the ground beneath. He couldn't believe the girl was still going.

The climb grew more technical and Farwick could feel the strain. His muscles started to quiver. The girl kept going, the red cooler flopping awkwardly until she disappeared over a ledge half way up the cliff face. Farwick forced himself higher, checking each handhold before trusting his weight to it. He was too old for this shit.

The girl couldn't climb beyond the ledge. He had her cornered.

He reached up, stuck his foot into a crevice and pushed himself onto the ledge.   The rock overhung the shelf, effectively keeping her from climbing higher.

She cowered on the far end of the shelf, knees wrapped against her heaving chest. Tears streamed down her face.

"Haven't you climbed into a pretty pickle? Give me the cooler, and I'll let you go," he said.

She squinted at him, but didn't answer. The cooler sat in front of her. He would have to crawl twenty feet across the ledge to reach it. The overhang made standing upright impossible. Farwick moved toward her, but she grabbed the cooler and held it over the side.

Farwick recoiled. "No! Don't drop that."

She set it down in front of her.

Farwick smiled. "A game, eh?" he sneered. "I love games."

She smeared tears from her face with her forearm. He looked down at the girl's friend and laughed. "Sorry about your friend." Farwick sat back to catch his breath. She wasn't going anywhere. The chill air sucked the sweat from his shirt, cooling him down.

He picked up a loose pebble and flicked it over the side. It gave him an idea. He worked several large pieces of shale loose from the rock beside him. He had the girl's attention.

He held the first out toward the girl, careful to highlight the jagged edge. "Why don't you give me that cooler before I drop this on your friend?"

She turned her head to the side, listening, but didn't respond. He shrugged again and pitched the sharp rock over the edge, watching it skip down the side like a spinning saw blade. The girl reacted. She grabbed hold of the overhang and leaned out to see. The shale glanced off the cliff face near the bottom and embedded itself into the ground not far from the boy's head like a primitive Chinese star.

Farwick looked at the girl. She grabbed the cooler and held it towards him. "I thought you'd see it my way," he said. He fought his way across the first fifteen feet of the narrow ledge on his hands and knees. "Bring it here. Carefully." He motioned to her. She would do exactly what he wanted. He was in control again.

She slid along on her bottom, scooting the cooler in front of her, but keeping her hands firmly on the strap. Almost there. The ledge narrowed and he reached out to grab it. The girl pulled it back toward her then launched it out over the side into the clear spring air.

The red cooler sailed beyond reach, its carrying handle flapping like a kite's tail as it sailed down toward the ground. Preston

Farwick leaned out to catch it. His knees tore loose and he felt his side smash on rock. The cliff face pulled away as if the whole world was moving and he was standing still.

His arms wind-milled. He saw the girl one last time; her eyes were closed.

Chapter 63

April 26

Ashley didn't look down. Couldn't. She didn't want to see Chase laying crumpled beside the body of The Moderator.

She curled up on the ledge, shivering with tears and cold and fear. The dizziness had abated, but the ringing wouldn't stop. She couldn't make it go away; couldn't hear anything else.

A movement beside her caught her eye. She brushed blurring tears aside. A rope dangled from overhead. Probably a climber repelling down the cliff face. Why they'd be here when everyone else was evacuating was beyond her.

Ashley curled in a ball and clung to the rock. Legs appeared, feet swinging free as the rock face opened to the ledge. The legs came to rest on the rock shelf and a man stooped down.

"Dad!" She couldn't believe it.

Sorrow was swallowed up by his embrace. The pain leaked out in her tears, streamed down her face and wet her dad's shoulder.

After a while, he pulled away and pointed to the rope. She shook her head. Ashley produced two six-inch thermoses from behind her. The red tape and bio hazard labels were enough to convince her dad not to open them. She'd pulled them from the cooler before the man made the ledge. There was no way she was going to let him have them, whatever they were. If he faked a nuclear event to get into the lab, then he was up to a whole new kind of crazy.

Her dad tucked the narrow thermoses inside his shirt front and buttoned it closed. He flicked the rope to Ashley and helped her maneuver off the ledge.

Once past the overhang, climbing was easy. At the top, she rolled onto flat rock and shook the rope. She'd made it. Then she recognized the rope as her own. Her dad must have found it in the car and driven around to the top of the cliff.

Chapter 64
April 26

They drove the short distance to the bottom of the cliff, ditched the vehicle by the boat launch and ran down the gravel line toward Chase. Ashley had never really seen her father run before. She knew he jogged for exercise, but this felt different.

A German shepherd materialized from the woods and ran along beside them. They kept going. It was already a day of the weird. The ringing in her ears surrounded everything. Ashley saw her mother leaning over Chase's body.

The dog ran ahead and sniffed at The Moderator. Her scruff bristled when it smelled death. She backed away, stiff legged and growling. It then moved to Chase and started licking his face clean.

Ashley knelt down beside her mother. Chase looked different without glasses. Like someone she recognized but hadn't seen in a while. She wondered if she'd ever really seen him before. A finger of blood trickled from behind his ear. She reached out and touched his face, afraid it would feel cold and dead.

Chase opened his eyes, blinked hard and smiled weakly. "Ashley?" Chase mumbled without moving his jaw. "Why are you crying?"

Ashley stifled a sob. "I was afraid I'd have to bring you flowers."

Chapter 65
April 30

"Ever been paid to work with computers?" Officer Ken Dixon looked at Ralph. The kid cut an unlikely figure as a hack.

"Nope. I only work on a pro bono basis," Ralph said with an air of superiority that collided badly with his green nail polish and black mascara.

"Perfect. Then we might be able to afford you," Dixon chuckled. "Remember. You're not allowed to touch anything unless they give you the all clear."

"Deal. Am I going to get in trouble?"

"I think you'll be okay. Considering you helped to find the bad guy. But you were playing with heady stuff." Dixon turned the cruiser up the driveway and parked in front of the garage.

The entire front lawn of Preston Farwick's house crawled with investigators. The Federal Bureau of Investigation assigned a Hazardous Evidence Response Team or HERTU to the case. Any crime involving nuclear incidents or weapons of mass destruction automatically moved up to the Federal level for investigation and HERTU served as the official liaison to local police.

The agent in charge of the scene strolled across the grass and shook Dixon's hand.

"Officer Dixon," she said. "A pleasure to meet you in person. I'm Angela Hart."

"Hi, Angela. This is Ralph." Dixon introduced the boy. "He and his friends were responsible for tracking down this guy. The other kids are recovering from injuries. The hospital is keeping them isolated just in case, but it doesn't look like they've been exposed to any biological agents. You should be able to talk to them in a few days.

"Good. We completed our threat credibility evaluation early this morning." Agent Hart nodded toward the front door and led them into the house. Ralph covered his nose with a hand. Here and there, red tags labeled pieces of furniture.

Agent Hunt smiled. "Don't worry. There's nothing scary in here."

"Where is his wife?" Dixon asked.

"According to our records, she's not in the state. Filed for divorce over a month ago," she replied.

"No kidding." Dixon shook his head. "You think you know a guy."

The agent led them past a cluster of men at the kitchen table working through the contents of a filing cabinet. They stepped into Farwick's office, and she motioned to the couch.

The office had a stale, un-aired smell about it, but the desk was in meticulous order.

"Funny thing," Dixon said. "His office at work was the antithesis of this. I always thought of him as a sloppy creative mind."

"Sloppy, no. Creative mind, well..." Agent Hunt sat in Farwick's chair.

"He was a friggin' genius," Ralph chimed in.

"Maybe," Hart conceded. "The man was exploiting a world we have yet to get our arms around as law enforcement. The pace of technological advancement has outstripped our capacity to police it. Our teams are good at cataloging chemical, biological, radiological and nuclear evidence, but this..." she gestured to the office and sighed. "This is just one guy, probably acting alone, who knows a little more about technology than most people around him. And there's no one to stop him from manipulating as many kids as he wants." Hart shook her head.

"Manipulation and blackmail are harder to clean up," Dixon said.

An agent knocked on the open door and walked in. "Hart, you've got to see this." He dropped a file in front of her. "I think this player got away with murder and framed his cousin." The agent checked his notepad for a name. "According to the pieces we're pulling together, this guy's cousin, Seth Mallory, was put away for life."

Chapter 66
May 5

The morning dawned with the first hint of summer sunshine. Puffy clouds cruised against a backdrop of perfect blue and the robins busily zigzagged over neighborhood lawns pulling at wormy strings.

Chase hadn't seen Ashley since everything happened. They'd both spent the first few days in bio-containment under plastic tents at a local hospital. The pain in his head subsided, but he still couldn't eat. The doctor wired his jaw back together. The slushy, applesauce, ice cream diet quickly lost its appeal and thoughts of eating real food rumbled around his stomach.

His mom came in to visit, but she couldn't smoke in the hospital, so she never stayed long. Pastor Blithe was his only regular. Maybe he was forgiven for getting Ashley involved in this mess. As a reverend, Philip could get in to see anyone. With a clerical collar and a black leather Bible, no one bothered to stop him. Chase wasn't sure how that worked, but he was glad for the company. He told Chase Ashley's hearing was improving, and they could talk to her without shouting.

After the hospital, Chase was interviewed by an FBI agent who turned out to be a normal person doing her job. He'd expected her to be a little more like the movies, but he should have known better.

Chase stood at the front door of the rectory and knocked. He felt nervous, but Pastor Philip told him to stop by after things settled down. Chase poked the spot between his nose where the glasses used to sit. Still getting used to the contacts.

Ashley stood with her hands curled up inside sweatshirt sleeves.

"What took you so long?" she asked.

Chase pointed at his jaw. "I've been a little busy." His lips moved, but his mouth didn't. "They've got me wired up."

Ashley looked behind her into the house. "You wanna take a walk?"

He nodded.

They set off down the sidewalk like so many times before, going a few blocks without talking, enjoying the warm and the sunshine.

"Oh. I brought something for you." Chase stopped and reached into his pocket.

"You sound like you have a mouth full of cotton," Ashley smiled.

Chase grunted and handed her a package.

Ashley tore open the tissue paper and stared at the remote control. "What's this?"

"That's so you can turn off the scary pictures in your mind when you wake up," Chase said. "It's the best solution I could think of while I was laying in the hospital."

She bit her lip again. "Thanks," she said. "You're sweet."

Oh hell, thought Chase. That's the last thing he wanted to be. Ashley's short, sweet, nerdy friend.

He kicked at a crack in the sidewalk.

Ashley pushed a button.

"What's that for?" Chase managed.

"Pause." She shrugged. "I don't want to move on from here yet."

"Why?" he asked.

She leaned in and kissed him. On the lips.

He didn't even have time to pucker.

"That's why," she said. And Ashley laughed.

Chase never heard such a wonderful sound.

Epilogue
June 5

This is not a game for sissies. CRETAN typed white words on a black screen. *Are you sure you want to play?*

Yes. The reply.

Prove it.

He had a player. His first real player. All so pathetically simple.

CRETAN sat back and stared at the screen, intoxicated by the power of anonymity.   He raised his arms. Green fingernails disappeared into triumphant fists.

"The Moderator lives!" he shouted.

Other books by Dwight Kopp

The Zambezi Chronicles
      The Contract*
      Critical Fault*
      Cover of Darkness

And

The Moderator Series
      The Moderator
      The Coma
      Grid Lock

Audio available from Audible.com or iTunes.com.

On Facebook at www.facebook.com/dwightkoppbooks

On the web at www.dwightkopp.com

Acknowledgments

Special thanks to Doe Kopp, Tiffani Rooney, Martha Squaresky, Jay Squaresky, and Rachel Reilly for their reading, edits and input. Any remaining errors are entirely my fault.

About the Author

Dwight Kopp lived (mostly) in Zambia, Africa until he was thirteen. His fondest memories include listening to the sound of elephants raiding the peanut fields as he drifted off to sleep. He now lives and writes in Lancaster County where he married the woman of his dreams. They have five (amazing) children.